As soon as night fell I drew the curtains, put on my night vision goggles and sat on my bed in the darkness, waiting.

Before long there was a scraping, shuffling noise, as if something too big to be moving about under my bed was moving about under my bed. Then came a horrible sniffing, like someone trying to suck a cheese-grater backwards through a hosepipe, and a deep, sinister, growling voice intoned:

"Fee fi fo fater! I smell the blood of a Monster Investigator!"

I smiled to myself.

"Very funny, Bernard," I said. "Ready to go?"

Also available by John Dougherty,
and published by Young Corgi Books:

JACK SLATER, MONSTER INVESTIGATOR
"Fabulously monstrous" www.writeaway.org.uk

ZEUS ON THE LOOSE!
"Energetic and page-turning" *INK magazine*

ZEUS TO THE RESCUE
"An instantly involving, constantly hilarious tale"
Andy Stanton, author of the Mr Gum series, in
Junior Education

NITERACY HOUR
"This book is unique . . . a great example of the quirky humour that younger readers enjoy"
Children's Books, Ireland

Published by Corgi Yearling Books:

BANSI O'HARA
AND THE BLOODLINE PROPHECY
"A romping good read . . . From the opening chapter we are hurled into a whirlwind of a story, full of humour, excitement, suspense and fantasy' *INIS*

For more information about John Dougherty:
www.visitingauthor.com

JOHN DOUGHERTY

JACK SLATER AND THE WHISPER OF DOOM

Illustrated by
Georgien Overwater

JACK SLATER AND THE WHISPER OF DOOM
A YOUNG CORGI BOOK 978 0 552 55805 1

Published in Great Britain by Young Corgi,
an imprint of Random House Children's Books
A Random House Group Company

This edition published 2009

1 3 5 7 9 10 8 6 4 2

The Random House Group Limited supports the Forest Stewardship Council (FSC), the leading international forest certification organization. All titles that are printed on Greenpeace-approved FSC-certified paper carry the FSC logo. Our paper procurement policy can be found at www.rbooks.co.uk/environment.

Set in Bembo MT Schoolbook 16/20pt
by Falcon Oast Graphic Art Ltd.

Young Corgi Books are published by Random House Children's Books,
61–63 Uxbridge Road, London W5 5SA,

www.**kidsatrandomhouse**.co.uk
www.**rbooks**.co.uk

Addresses for companies within the Random House Group Limited can be found at:
www.randomhouse.co.uk/offices.htm

THE RANDOM HOUSE GROUP Limited Reg. No. 954009

A CIP catalogue record for this book is available from the British Library.

Printed in the UK by CPI Bookmarque, Croydon, CR0 4TD

As always, for the wonderful little monsters who live in my house and who seem to be getting bigger and bigger . . .

Home | FAQ | Contact us

Monsters under the bed? It needn't be a problem!

If you have a serious monster-under-the-bed infestation, you need to call the professionals. But for the common, everyday monster appearances, here are a few tips:

1. Fight fright with light. Keep a torch handy. Catch a monster in its beam, and the creature will vanish.

2. Be ready with a teddy. A well-loved cuddly toy, blanket or snuggly is a terrific weapon against monsters. Make sure you've got one in bed with you – a teddy, not a monster – and give it lots of love and cuddles to charge it up.

3. Use your head when you go to bed. Most of the stuff kids make up to keep monsters away actually works – tricks like counting to five as you get into bed, for instance, or hiding under the bedclothes.

For more info, see our FAQ page, or leave a question in our guestbook. And remember – there are no monster problems that can't be solved!

Search this site [ ] Go

I crept cautiously round the corner, adjusting my night vision goggles as I went. The monster underworld is not somewhere you want to hang around, and I'd been spending much too much time passing through there lately; it was starting to creep me out.

There was no sign of movement in the narrow corridor. Just in case, my hand went to my torch.

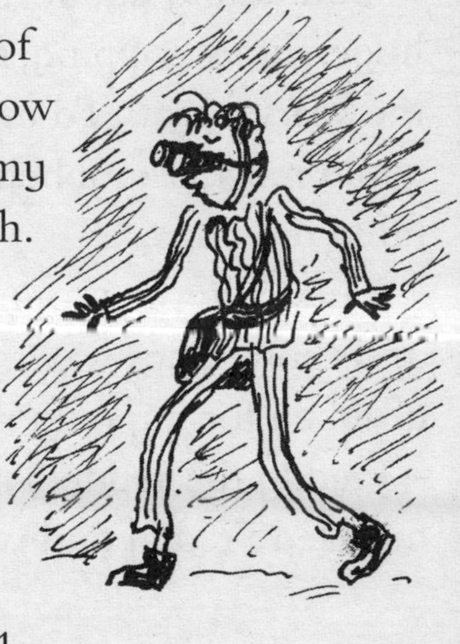

It wasn't there.

I knew I'd brought it with me. I was sure I hadn't dropped it; but however it had happened, I didn't have it now. Not for the first time, I was thankful I'd started carrying a spare.

Except – this time, it seemed, I wasn't. That pocket was empty, too.

"Cherry," I whispered to my partner, "can I use your spare torch?"

She didn't answer. I turned to get her attention, and instead got the shock of my life.

She wasn't there either. But something else was.

Something about fifty metres high, with huge, slime-dripping, razor-sharp fangs and the worst breath I'd ever smelled. Before I could react, it grabbed me by the collar and lifted me up.

Suddenly the ground was too far away, and those fangs were way too close. I grabbed for my only remaining weapon – Freddy the Teddy. The monster roared; I fumbled Freddy and watched him slip and

fall to the floor below. I was defenceless.

The monster laughed, an evil, chilling cackle. It lifted me higher, until I was staring into its wicked little piggy eyes. Then it spoke, blowing the foul stink of its breath over my face.

"Jack Slater," it rumbled, "what's fifteen take away ten?"

I blinked, and stared at it. Generally speaking, monsters like to hear children scream. They're not that interested in making them do sums. In fact, on most monsters' lists of hobbies, I'd have guessed maths ranked only slightly above sunbathing.

"Oh, come on, Jack," it growled. "It's not that difficult!"

I shook myself, suddenly realizing what was happening. "Five!" I blurted out as the monster's face shrank and changed. Behind it, tables, chairs, kids and an interactive whiteboard blurred out of nothing and snapped into focus; and suddenly I was wide awake and staring into the face of Mr Ashford, the deputy head. Nothing was left of the monster.

Well, nothing except the little piggy eyes and bad breath.

"Honestly, Jack!" Mr Ashford said. "If your eyes hadn't been open just now, I'd have thought you were asleep!"

I ignored the giggles of my classmates as Mr Ashford returned to the lesson. I ignored the lesson, too; I had more important things to think about.

It wasn't altogether surprising that I'd ended up falling asleep in class. The monsters had been unusually active lately, and Cherry and I had been kept very busy. Which meant, among other things, that I wasn't getting enough sleep at night.

Nor was it odd that I'd fallen asleep with my eyes open. As a Monster Investigator – let's not be modest, as the world's *greatest* Monster Investigator – I'd developed something of an instinct for self-preservation.

No, what troubled me was the nightmare. I don't *do* nightmares. Well, not about monsters, anyway. My worst dreams usually involve things like being locked in a room made entirely of pink sparkly books about fairies, and having to read my way out.

But this wasn't the first time lately that I'd had a bad dream about the monster underworld, and it was beginning to rattle me. I mean, in real life, the monsters never won. Never. Never had, never would. Not against me.

But for them to start winning in my dreams . . . it didn't feel right. It didn't feel good at all.

When I got home, the first thing I did was to check our website – 'our' meaning *Slater and Jackson, Freelance Monster Investigators*. The 'Slater' part is me, of course, and the 'Jackson' part is Cherry Jackson, my best friend and the world's second-greatest Monster Investigator – though according to Cherry I'm second-greatest and she's first.

Cherry and I have been working together ever since we met on a mission in the monster underworld, which turned out to be the biggest case I'd ever taken on - and which ended up with both of us resigning from the Ministry of Monsters' roster of official Monster Investigators and going freelance. When we did that, we decided it would be a good idea to let other kids know about us online; and sure enough, every now and again someone would add something to the guest book that proved to be worth investigating.

Like today, for example. In amongst all the usual stuff about funny noises coming from downstairs in the evening (which inevitably turned out to be grown-ups watching TV), and the not-very-funny comments from teenagers about 'there's a monster in my house, can you get rid of it, it's my little brother', there was something which looked interesting, in a weird sort of way.

It was from a kid calling himself Mousetrap, complaining about monsters hiding in his wardrobe. That's not so unusual in itself; it's not unheard of for monsters to creep out from under someone's bed while they're asleep, hide in the nearest cupboard and wake them up by making spooky noises. Once the kid in question is thoroughly awake, they jump out and roar. What was odd, though, was that these monsters sounded as if they were hiding *from* something.

Every night for the past three nights, Mousetrap had been woken in the middle of the night by strange noises coming from the wardrobe.

Some kids, if this happened, would do the sensible thing and snuggle up beneath the bedclothes, pulling them over their heads

– what we Monster Investigators call the Hedgehog Position. To the average monster, the Hedgehog Position looks like an empty bed. If you keep still and stay under the covers, it'll get bored and go away within minutes.

Other kids would do the brave thing. They'd grab a torch, go to the wardrobe and look in. If the torchlight hits the monster – *poof*, it vanishes.

Mousetrap, after two nights of doing the sensible thing, had done what I can only describe as the stupid thing. His curiosity had got the better of him, and he'd gone to the wardrobe unarmed and opened the door.

There, inside the wardrobe, were a number of monsters – Mousetrap reckoned five, on the grounds that he'd seen five pairs of eyes staring at him. This showed me he didn't know much about monsters – most creatures may have two eyes each, but with monsters, you can never tell. It could have been ten monsters with one eye, one monster with ten eyes, or any one of a dozen other combinations.

Anyway, the important thing is that

when he opened the door, instead of leaping out and roaring at him, the monsters all screamed.

Specifically, they screamed, "Shut the door! Shut the door!"

Not unnaturally, Mousetrap was a little puzzled by this. So he'd done a web-search on monsters in bedrooms and come up with our website, and he wondered if we could advise him.

You bet we could. In fact, we could do more than advise; we could investigate. All we had to do was hitch a lift.

With a monster.

As soon as night fell I drew the curtains, put on my night vision goggles and sat on my bed in the darkness, waiting.

Before long there was a scraping, shuffling noise, as if something too big to be moving about under my bed was moving about under my bed. Then came a horrible sniffing, like someone trying to suck a cheese-grater backwards through a hosepipe, and a deep, sinister, growling voice intoned:

"Fee fi fo fater!
I smell the blood
of a Monster
Investigator!"

I smiled to myself.

"Very funny, Bernard," I said. "Ready to go?"

Bernard sighed and wriggled out from under the bed, unfurling his long downy ears as he stood. "Doesn't *anything* ever scare you, Jack?" he asked.

I grinned. "You know me, Bernard," I said, hopping down to floor level. "Utterly fearless."

Poor old Bernard. Even if I *was* the type to scare easily, I doubt if he'd be able to frighten me. He's probably the least scary monster I've ever seen. He's probably the least scary monster *anyone's* ever seen. The number of people who've ever been afraid of him can probably be counted on the fingers of one finger.

He's a good friend, though, and my best source of information about what goes on in the monster underworld. He's also very handy for getting about.

“One day, Jack,” he said. “One day, I’ll see what you look like when you’re frightened.” Then he did a double take. “What’s that you’re wearing?”

“They’re called ‘clothes’,” I told him. “This is what I wear during the daytime.”

“The top doesn’t match the bottom!” he said. “That’s so weird!”

I looked up at him – two metres of cuddly bunny rabbit covered in soft fluffy feathers – and decided not to say anything about what was weird and what wasn’t. “Come on,” I said. “Cherry’ll be waiting. She’ll be wearing clothes, too.”

“What’s wrong with pyjamas?” he

muttered. "You *always* wear pyjamas when you're investigating."

What was wrong with pyjamas was that we were going to meet Mousetrap. If his mum caught us it was going to be difficult enough explaining why two strange children were in her son's room after his bed time, without having to explain the fact that we were dressed for a sleepover.

I picked up my backpack – containing all the kit I'd normally keep in the pockets of my Night Operations Utility Pyjamas – and followed Bernard into the darker darkness beneath the bed, trying to ignore the shiver down my spine that came as the carpet under my fingers began to wriggle and squirm. I should have been used to that feeling by now, but part of me was still thinking about the nightmare I'd had in class. Thankfully, we weren't planning on staying in the monster underworld – just passing through one of the quiet bits on the way to Cherry's house.

Cherry was waiting for us, her huge Night Blaster torch at the ready, her Mr Piggy backpack on her back. She looked different from usual; it took me a moment to realize it was the clothes. She's got some great outfits for active duty – combat nighties, camouflage pyjamas, that sort of thing – but I'd never seen her in plain old jeans and sweatshirt before. She still looked cool, I guess, but I wasn't used to it.

Her hair looked different, too; she'd got it plaited into cornrows, with a small, brightly coloured bead on the end of each one. One thing that hadn't changed, though, was her trademark grin. Cherry has the biggest, most cheerful smile of anyone I've ever met,

and probably the brightest, whitest teeth, too.

"Hey, guys," she said. "Ready to go?"

We dropped down on all fours and followed Bernard, keeping close as he squeezed himself under the bed and back into the monster underworld. The fact that monsters can do this – move from the monster underworld to the darkness under your bed and back again – can be pretty irritating to a Monster Investigator, but if you happen to be friends with a monster like Bernard it can also be a handy way of getting from place to place. It would be even handier if we didn't have to go through the monster underworld, but you can't have everything. So through the underworld we went, and minutes later we emerged under Mousetrap's bed.

Cherry and I squeezed ourselves out and sprang to our feet. Bernard stayed hidden; Mousetrap sounded like a pretty cool customer, but we didn't want to risk freaking him out. Nor, for that matter, did we want to risk him putting the light on without thinking and sending Bernard off to the Great Space-Under-the-Bed in the Sky.

The room was dark, but not completely – there was just about enough of a glow through a chink in the curtains to be able to make out one another's faces, even when we slipped our goggles off. It was also nicely monster-free, which is just how I like bedrooms to be. At first glance it appeared to be Mousetrap-free, too, but a quick look at the bed suggested otherwise.

"Nice Hedgehog Position, Mousetrap," I said, "but you can come out now." After a pause, during which the lump in the bed didn't move, I said, "It's me – Jack Slater. I emailed you earlier."

A face peeked out cautiously, and then grinned at us. Its owner sat up, flinging the duvet off.

"Hi," he said.

"Hi, Mousetrap."

"It's Sunil," he told us. "'Mousetrap' is just the name I use on the web."

"Well, pleased to meet you," I told him. "This is my associate, Cherry Jackson."

"Hi," Cherry said, flashing him a dazzling smile. "Nice room."

"So," I said, "these monsters: any idea why they're hiding?"

Sunil shook his head.

"Or why they picked your wardrobe to hide in?"

"Nope."

"Or why they keep coming back?"

Sunil looked blank. "Coming back?"

"You said you'd been woken three nights in a row."

"Oh – yes, that's right; but I don't think they came back."

Cherry frowned. "Do you mean you think it's different monsters each time?"

Sunil shook his head again. "No, it's the same ones. I just don't think they went away."

Cherry and I looked at each other. "Sunil," Cherry said, "are you saying you had monsters in your wardrobe for *two and a half days*?"

Sunil nodded. "More like three, now."

My mouth almost fell open with surprise as I realized what he meant. "Hold on," I said. "Are you telling me they're *still there*?"

Sunil looked puzzled. "Well – yeah, of course. That's why I called you guys in. I've been wearing the same clothes since Monday, and my mum's going to

insist I put on something clean tomorrow. You do get rid of monsters, don't you?"

"Course we do," Cherry said. "There's nobody better than us at getting rid of monsters."

"It's just that they don't normally stay where they are and wait for us to do it," I added.

"So what's your plan?" Sunil asked. "Are you going to blast them?"

"I think maybe we should find out what they're doing here," Cherry said.

I nodded. "It could be dangerous," I told Sunil. "You might be best adopting the Hedgehog Position. You'll be safest that way."

"And miss all the fun?" he retorted. "Not likely!"

I had to hand it to him, he was a gutsy little guy.

"OK," I said, "if that's how you want to play it, that's fine by me. But you've got to do exactly what I tell you . . ."

Cherry coughed meaningfully.

". . . exactly what *we* tell you," I went on, "and you'll need to be kitted out. Take this." I handed him my spare torch, a slim, sleek number with a rubberized grip. Cherry was already reaching into Mr Piggy, her trusty backpack, and pulling out her spare pair of night vision goggles for Sunil. I went to the curtains and drew them tight, shutting out the glow from outside.

"Wow," Sunil murmured, as we slipped on the goggles and the room took on a green glow. "Cool!"

As everything slid smoothly into focus, I looked up at the wardrobe that dominated Sunil's bedroom. It was huge. I guessed that if I was a bunch of monsters looking for a hiding place, I might well have chosen this one, too.

Cherry took up position on one side of the wardrobe door, torch at the ready, looking every inch the professional, and nodded at me. "Let's go, partner. I've got you covered."

Sunil stood on the other side, waving my spare torch around like a complete amateur, and added, "Me too!"

"Um . . . maybe you should stand back a bit?" I suggested.

Sunil looked offended. "This is how they always do it in the movies!" he pointed out.

"That's true," Cherry agreed; and she

should know. I've never met anyone who's seen as many films as she has. "But there's a difference, Sunil. In the movies, when the cops stand either side of a door, they're about to enter an apartment or a hotel room. Whereas this is a wardrobe."

"So?" Sunil pouted. "What's your point?"

"My point is," Cherry explained patiently, "that wardrobe doors open outwards, instead of inwards. So if you're standing there when this one opens, it's likely to smack you in the face."

Sunil thought about this. Then he smiled an enthusiastic little smile and moved behind me. Right behind me. I could practically feel him breathing on my shoulder blades.

"OK," he said. "I'll stand here."

I rolled my eyes. Sunil was brave, all right, but he didn't have much sense where monsters were concerned – and absolutely no experience, either.

"And what happens," I asked, "if the monsters come rushing out and I have to jump backwards to get out of their way?"

He thought about this.

"How about here?" he asked, moving next to Cherry. And then moving sideways, a little away from her. And a little more. And a little more.

I gave him the nod when I reckoned he was standing where he couldn't do any harm.

"OK," I said to Cherry. She reached sideways and knocked on the door. There was a muffled "Eeek!" from inside, and a lot of shushing.

Cherry knocked again. "Open up!" she said. "It's the Monster Investigators!"

There was a lot of noisy shuffling, and

then a voice growled, "Go away!"

Cherry knocked again. "Listen here, monsters!" she commanded. "We are fully trained, highly professional and extremely dangerous Monster Investigators! We are armed! We have you surrounded! Throw down your weapons!"

There was a pause, and then a second voice asked nervously, "What if we don't have any weapons?"

Cherry sighed. She has a real sense of the dramatic, and she hates it when the monsters don't play along. "Just come out with your hands up, OK?"

There was another pause, and then the same voice said, "What if we don't have any hands?"

Cherry rolled her eyes. "Hands, tentacles, claws – whatever! Just put them up and come out!"

There was the sound of murmuring, and then the voice said, "What if someone's got claws *and* tentacles? I mean, which do you want them to put up . . . ?"

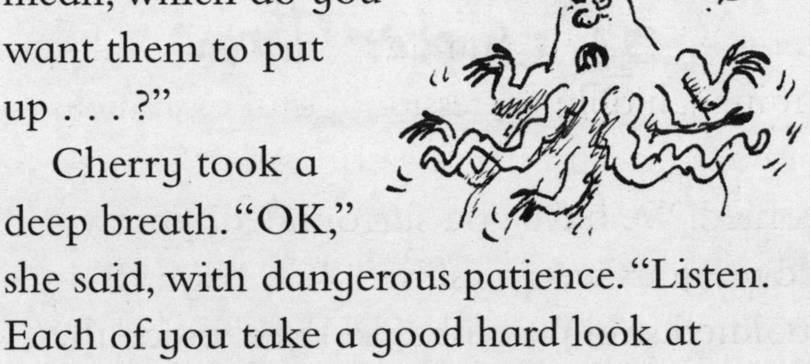

Cherry took a deep breath. "OK," she said, with dangerous patience. "Listen. Each of you take a good hard look at yourself. Identify the limbs you normally use to walk on. Then take all the limbs that are left over, put them up, and come out quietly before I lose my temper!"

Another pause; and then the first voice growled, "No. Go away."

Cherry looked at me and shook her head. I knew what she meant: plan A wasn't working. Time to go to plan B.

She stood back and pointed the huge reflector of her Night Blaster 35 squarely at the wardrobe door.

I grabbed the handle and pulled.

"Freeze!" Cherry snarled. The Night Blaster pointed straight at the darkness inside the wardrobe where the monsters crouched.

I've got to admit: if I was a monster, I'd have stopped dead at the sight of that huge torch in the hands of someone as mean-looking as Cherry was just then. I'd have frozen like an ice cube with frostbite, and then I'd have slowly raised everything – hands, tentacles, claws, feet, you name it. I'd even have raised the monster next to me if I'd thought it would help.

Not these guys. As soon as the door opened, they all began shrieking great panicky shrieks. If there'd been room in the wardrobe, I reckon they'd all have been running around like headless chickens.

Come to think of it, one of them *looked* kind of like a headless chicken.

But as mean as Cherry and her Night Blaster looked, it wasn't her they were scared of. And though I'd like to think that my reputation as the world's greatest Monster Investigator had preceded me, it wasn't me they were scared of either.

A brief chill of fear scuttled down my spine. What could have terrified these monsters so much that they'd hide in a wardrobe for three days? What could be so horrifying to them that just the thought of it was worse than the torches that were actually pointing at their heads? Or, in the case of those without heads, at the nearest equivalents.

"Close the door! Close the door!" the monsters screamed; and no matter how I tried to calm them down, no matter how Cherry waved her torch, they just wouldn't shut up.

And then there was a knock on the door.

Not the door I was holding, though it took me a second to realize it. Someone was knocking on Sunil's bedroom door.

I shut the wardrobe quickly but quietly. The monsters shut up. Sunil scampered back to his bed and threw himself under the covers; Cherry and I shrank into the shadows and made ourselves as small as we could.

The knock came again, and a woman's voice said, "Sunil?" Then came the click of the door softly opening, and she stepped inside. The light from the landing shone in, laying down a path that shone right to Sunil's bed. I hoped Bernard had had the sense to shuffle backwards.

"What was that noise, Sunil?" the woman asked, her slippers making no noise on the carpet as she padded over to his bed.

Sunil looked up at her with big, wide eyes. "I was just playing a story CD, Mum," he said. "Was it a bit loud?"

This kid was good. He almost had *me* convinced.

Sunil's mum laughed. "A bit loud? No – not for the man at the end of the road. For the rest of the street, though, I think it might have been." Her face wrinkled up in puzzlement. "What kind of story CD has all those horrible noises in it, anyway?" I held my breath, afraid we'd been rumbled; but then she went on: "No, don't tell me – one of those terrible Roald Dahl stories, I'll bet. Why can't you listen to something nice and gentle about ponies and kittens?"

Sunil smiled. "Come off it, Mum. Naanii told me you loved *Charlie and the Chocolate Factory* when you were my age."

His mum smiled back. "Well, maybe I did. But not at bed time!" She leaned over and kissed his forehead. Just for a second, his eyes flicked over to where we crouched, hidden in the shadow of the wardrobe. "I'm going to check back in fifteen minutes, and I expect you to be fast asleep!"

Sunil snuggled down under the covers and closed his eyes. But as soon as his mum pulled the door closed behind her, he was out of bed and coming across the carpet towards us, where he shuffled in a slightly embarrassed manner.

"Um . . . she doesn't usually kiss me goodnight," he began.

I cut him off. "Doesn't she? She should."

He stared at me. He hadn't been expecting that one, not from a big, tough Monster Investigator.

Cherry backed me up. "Jack's right – a goodnight kiss is a powerful protection against monsters. Gives them the creeps."

"Doesn't have to be from your mum, of course," I added. "Could be your dad, grandma, grandpa, guardian, carer . . ."

"Big sister, little brother, auntie, uncle," Cherry went on. "As long as it's a real kiss, from someone who loves you, it'll help keep monsters away."

Sunil's face puckered up in a frown. "But I thought you had be tough to deal with monsters!"

I nodded. "You do. So?"

"You think Clint Eastwood's mum never kissed him goodnight?" Cherry asked.

Sunil looked blank. "Who?"

Cherry grinned and shook her head. "Kids these days," she said. "What *do* they teach them in these schools? Anyway, guys, we've got some monsters to investigate."

"Yeah," I said, "but without bringing Sunil's mum back upstairs. What do you think – can we get the monsters to shut up when we open the door?"

Cherry shook her head. "They're scared stiff of something – so much so, they hardly noticed the Night Blaster. And if we can't hold the door open without them carrying on like a bunch of baboons, there's no way they're going to come out and answer questions quietly."

"That's my thinking," I said. "So there's only one option. I'm going to have to go in."

Cherry raised an eyebrow. "Oh yeah?

How come *you* get to be the one who goes in? And before you tell me it's because you're the world's greatest Monster Investigator, let me tell you that title's still very much in dispute as far as I'm concerned!"

I grinned at her. Sometimes she can read me like a book. One with very big pictures in full colour.

"OK," I said, "try this for size: in a confined space like that wardrobe, this" – I held up my compact torch – "is going to be easier to keep pointed at those monsters than *that*." I indicated the Night Blaster. "On the other hand, the thought of you ready to rip the door open and light up the inside of the wardrobe like the world's biggest sunbed is likely to keep them on their best behaviour." When she still didn't look convinced, I added, "And anyway, I thought of it first, so there!"

She sighed, moved to the wardrobe, and knocked on the door.

"Go away!" growled a voice.

Cherry ignored it. "OK, monsters, here's the deal," she said. "My partner's coming in. He's going to close the door behind him so you can go on hiding while he talks to you. Now, he's armed, but if you're good little monsters then his torch stays off. Any bad behaviour, though, and on go the lights.

"Meantime, I'm going to be standing out here with a torch the size of a car headlight, and if my partner isn't out of there in five minutes, completely unharmed, the last thought any of you have will be, 'Gosh, isn't it bright all of a sudden!' Got it?"

There was a pause, and then the voice growled, "Go away!"

Cherry looked at me. "Are you sure you want to do this, Jack? They may be complete wusses, but they're still monsters. And there's no bed in there to get into."

"You got a better idea?"

She shook her head. "You be careful in there, Jack Slater," she said.

"I'll be fine," I said, more bravely than I felt.

"Course you will," she told me. "You've got the world's greatest Monster Investigator watching your back." She winked, and grinned at me.

I grinned back. "Yeah, the world's greatest – after me!"

I reached into my backpack and pulled out Freddy the Teddy, tucking him under my arm. Then I opened the wardrobe door and, before the monsters had time to start up with the shrieking again, I stepped inside and closed the door behind me.

Chapter Four

The monsters cowered away from me, all of them keeping their eyes fixed on the torch – or at least, all of them that had eyes, although the headless-chickeny one somehow seemed to be staring with its neck.

"Go away!" growled the one that kept growling "go away". Obviously a monster of few growls. It was a runty little thing that looked like a squashed hamster with toothache. I gestured casually with the torch and it shrank back into the corner, muttering something I didn't quite catch, though I'd be willing to bet it was, "Go away."

"OK, Monster Investigator," spat another voice. I made out a dark shadow of a creature, stretched against one wall of the wardrobe like the wallpaper of your nightmares, given away only by three blinking eyes and the flashing of its mouth as it spoke. "You be safe if we be safe. What you want?"

I took a deep breath, and straight away wished I hadn't. The wardrobe smelled strongly of monster – a stuffy, humid odour that made me think of wet dog and cheap cola with just a hint of shoe polish. It would have been much worse if I'd closed the door completely, but I'd figured I might need to get out in a hurry. Anyway, even without monsters around it's not safe shutting yourself in a wardrobe. Just ask C. S. Lewis. Now *there* was a guy who knew about wardrobe safety.

"What you want?" the wallpapery one asked again. I looked it straight in the eye, and then, just for good measure, in the other two as well.

"Information," I told it.

"Go away," muttered the squashed hamster.

I gave it the eyeball. "You," I told it, wagging Freddy at it, "are looking for a mouthful of teddy." It shut up again.

"What kind of information?" asked Wallpaper, who seemed to have elected itself spokesthing for the group.

"Well, specifically I'd like to know what you monsters are so scared of . . ."

"Scared?" Wallpaper bristled. "I ain't scared of nothing."

"That's not how it looks to me," I said. "You've been hiding in here for three days, shrieking in panic at anyone who opens the door. That's not normal. I mean – why haven't you gone back to the monster underworld?"

The wardrobe trembled slightly as the monsters all shuddered.

"It not safe," the squashed-looking runty one mumbled, proving it knew at least three more words. "Go away," it added, proving it hadn't forgotten the first two.

"What do you mean, not safe?" I demanded. "What could be less safe for a bunch of monsters than hiding in a wardrobe during the day? What if someone opened the door?"

"Why should we tell you?" came a nervous growl from over in the darkest corner.

I looked at the warty beast that had spoken. It was a dumpy little thing with soft, spongy-looking crab-claws. *And* tentacles; little ones on top of its head.

"Because I've got a big torch," I told it. "And because my friend's got a *really* big torch. And because if you tell us what we want to know we might leave them switched off."

Warty cleared its throat. Or throats; it was hard to tell.

"OK," it muttered. "All right. But you got to promise us something."

"No deals, monster," I said. "Tell us what we want to know, behave yourselves, and the torches stay off. That's it."

The monster shifted uncomfortably. "Um, yeah, well, that's good," it said, "but the thing is . . . we might not want the torches to stay off."

I stared at it. Most monsters are pretty thick, but they all understand that light is deadly to them.

"The thing is," it went on, "what we're scared of . . . well, if it finds us – if it catches us . . ." It looked around at the other monsters for support. All of them nodded their heads. Except for the headless-chickeny one, which sort of nodded its neck. Yeucchhh.

"If it catches us," Warty said again, "we'd rather face the torch. We want you to promise that if it finds us here, you'll turn the lights on it. Even if you get us, too."

"Are you serious?" I asked; but I knew the answer already. "If that's what you want, you've got yourselves a deal. But first I need to know what it is you're scared of."

The monsters looked at each other in a you-tell-him-no-you-tell-him kind of way. Warty nudged Runty; Runty nudged Wallpaper. Wallpaper nudged Runty back. Runty shook its squashed little head and nudged Warty. Warty blinked nervously, five bloodshot eyes flashing one after the other and then all together like some kind of tasteless Christmas decoration.

Finally, one of them spoke up.

Unfortunately, it was the headless chicken.

"Mmmmng," it said expressively. "Mmm mmmmmmh mmmngmngmmmmng mmmmmmnh. Mmmmm mmmmng mmmmmgnmmmmmh—"

"Hang on," I said. "Sorry to interrupt, and not meaning to be rude or anything, but the deal is that you tell me what's going on in words I can understand. This 'mmm mmm mmm' stuff just doesn't fit the bill."

The creature did that staring-with-its-neck thing again, and I realized I might have offended it.

"'Doesn't fit the bill' is just an expression," I told it. "It doesn't mean you have to *have* a bill – or a beak of any sort . . ."

The neck looked away, insulted. I think. It was kind of hard to tell.

I sighed. "Listen, monsters," I said, "there's a kid outside who'd like to get into some clean clothes. So, are you going to tell me what's bothering you, or do we have to do this the hard way?"

The monsters looked at each other, and for a moment I was worried they were going to start that whole nudging thing again, but then Warty shuffled forward.

"OK," it said, lowering its voice. "OK. What it is, see . . . what it is, is that something came after us."

My patience was really wearing thin. "Yeah, I'd got that," I said. "The question is, what?"

Warty shook its head. "No. The question is, where? Where did it come from? You see . . . " It edged closer, dropping its voice to a whisper. "The Dark Depths are open!"

"The what?" I asked.

Warty shifted uneasily. "The Dark Depths," it began. "They're—"

But before it could say any more, there was a sound from outside the wardrobe. I heard Cherry call out, a cry of surprise and anger that was suddenly cut off. Someone pulled the door open behind me.

The wardrobe was flooded with light. The monsters vanished without trace.

My night vision goggles flared, bright and white, in the sudden light. Jamming my torch into my pocket, I pushed them up off my eyes and turned to find myself staring into the last face on earth I wanted to see.

Clyde Pumfrey-Soames. Spoilt rich kid, Minister for Monsters, and one-time traitor to the whole human race.

"Slater," he sneered. "I might have known."

"You knew, Clyde," I said, stepping forward into the brightly lit room. He moved back, nervous all of a sudden. "You had a few clues, for a start – like the fact that you have my partner there." I nodded over to where some burly, stupid-looking kid – one of Clyde's henchmen – was holding Cherry tightly, one hand over her mouth, obviously to stop her warning me. Sunil was standing nearby, looking nervous, clearly not sure what to do. "You can let go of her now, Fatso," I told him. "I already know you're here."

The big guy clearly wasn't used to thinking for himself. He looked at Clyde for the OK. Clyde nodded at him. "But watch

her, Smithers," he added. "Now, Slater, mind telling me what you're doing here?"

"I could ask you the same question," I retorted. "How did you know there was anything going on here tonight? Been spying on our website?"

He blushed. "The Ministry of Monsters has its methods, Slater – ones that we're not prepared to reveal to *ex*-Investigators. Now, I must insist that you tell me everything you've found out."

I glared at him. "I'm not telling you a thing – except that I'd have found out a lot more if you hadn't come bursting in with lights blazing. There were four monsters in there who were about to tell me something important when you wiped them out."

"Oh, come on now, Slater – you don't believe you can get anything worthwhile out of a monster, do you?"

"Why not, Clyde? You got quite a lot out of them. Of course, you had to promise them something in return."

Clyde blushed again, and glanced at Smithers. Clearly his pet thug didn't know his master's guilty past. Quickly, Clyde turned to Sunil and changed the subject.

"Anyway, Mr Mousetrap, there's your little problem solved. Just turn on the lights – that soon sorts them out. Sorry you were bothered by these cowboys. Next time," he went on, handing Sunil a card, "come straight to the experts."

"Experts!" Cherry scoffed. "The only thing you're an expert at, Clyde, is making a fool of yourself. Coming in here waving your official pass about like you're somebody special! And you watch it," she added, pointing at Smithers, whose little brain was beginning to catch up with the conversation and clearly wasn't liking what it was hearing. "You took me by surprise that time, buster; you won't be so lucky again!"

Clyde puffed himself up like one of those

ugly fish. "I'll thank you both to remember that I'm a government minister!" he pouted.

"Only because your daddy foots all the bills," I pointed out.

"It's not a *real* ministry, anyway," Cherry added.

"Be that as it may," Clyde went on in his most self-important manner, "it doesn't seem that either of you are being terribly helpful here, so I'm going to have to take you back to the Ministry of Monsters and question you there."

I laughed. "No chance, Clyde."

"Oh, I think there is, Slater. I think there's every chance." He turned towards the door. "Murgatroyd!" he called.

The door opened and Murgatroyd came in, closing it carefully behind him. He was the kind of kid who made Smithers look like a bit of a wimp. Imagine a two-legged rhinoceros in a school uniform and you'll get the picture. I found myself wondering whether a mouthful of teddy would work on him.

"Murgatroyd, Smithers," Clyde went on pompously, "Slater and Jackson will be coming with us. Don't use *too* much more force than you need to."

Murgatroyd, clearly no more of a thinker than Smithers, advanced threateningly on Sunil.

Clyde tutted. "No, no, Murgatroyd, that's

the client. We're taking these two."

"Forget it, Clyde," I said, acting braver than I felt. "We're going home."

"How do you plan on doing that?" he asked scornfully. "Come to that, how did you get in here in the first place?"

I guessed how Clyde had got in. He'd pulled up in his dad's chauffeur-driven limo, waved his official papers about and swanned in like he owned the place, telling Sunil's mum some nonsense about knowing her son at school. Probably he'd brought his dad with him to distract her and had left him downstairs, boasting to her about his important little government-minister son and stopping her from coming upstairs and spoiling his fun. It was good news that he hadn't guessed about our own method of transportation.

"None of your business, Clyde," I said. "But we're about to take the same route out of here – right, Cherry?"

"No you're not, Slater. Deal with them, boys!"

Smithers and Murgatroyd cracked their knuckles threateningly and lumbered towards us. But what they didn't know – and Clyde was forgetting – was that while they might be bigger than us, they weren't half the size of some of the monsters we'd tackled together. And probably not much brighter.

I tapped my goggles – still up on my forehead – and nodded my head towards the light switch by the door. Cherry got it at once.

"OK, pea-brains," I said, adopting my best karate-expert crouch. "Let's see what you're made of."

This was a risky thing to do, not least because I don't know the first thing about karate. Well, maybe the first thing. I know how to spell it. But that's about it.

It made them stop, though. They both

stared at me.

"What are you waiting for?" Clyde squawked. "Don't tell me you're scared of him! You're both twice his size!"

"We can handle the kid," Murgatroyd said. "But that bear of his is scary!" He snickered.

Now it was my turn to blush. I'd forgotten I was holding Freddy. I tucked him by one leg into my back pocket and took up the stance again, but somehow I couldn't help feeling that I'd lost the air of menace I was going for.

Smithers and Murgatroyd grinned

nastily at me and flexed their muscles. Which, though a trifle scary, was fine by me, since all the attention I was getting meant nobody was paying any attention to Cherry. She sprinted for the door and opened it.

"Murgatroyd!" squealed Clyde. "The girl! She's getting away, you twit!"

With a bellow of rage – or possibly just of stupidity – Murgatroyd put his head down and raced after Cherry. For such a big guy, he was fast. At that speed, he'd have caught her before she reached the stairs.

Cherry froze in the doorway, looking terrified. Which would have given the game away if Murgatroyd had known her like I do. Cherry doesn't do terrified.

In a single movement, an instant before he reached her, she stepped aside, slammed the door shut and coolly flicked the light switch.

Everything went dark. There was a

noise that sounded like something very hard and made of wood – at a guess, the door – being struck sharply by something very hard and made of wood – at a guess, Murgatroyd's head. I slipped my goggles back over my eyes and took in the scene.

It was very gratifying. Murgatroyd was lying in a crumpled heap in front of the door, completely blocking it. Smithers was groping his way around the room blindly, trying to find someone to deal with; but since Cherry and Sunil had both slipped their goggles on again, the only person he was lucky enough to blunder into was Clyde. Clyde tried to call him off, but found it rather difficult with both of Smithers' hands wrapped tightly round his throat.

"I got one, boss!" Smithers grunted. "What'll I do with him?"

"Cccchhhhhh!" Clyde suggested. "Ukkk-kkk-kkk!!!"

"Uh, you still there, boss?" Smithers asked. A trace of doubt crept its way across his Neanderthal expression as it occurred to him that out of five other people in the room, there were only two he had permission to strangle. You could almost see him struggling with the mental arithmetic. After a moment, he relaxed his grip just enough to let Clyde breathe.

Clyde sucked in a huge gasp of air. "You idiot, Smithers!" he coughed. Smithers let go of him – a little reluctantly, I thought – and turned, arms outstretched, to grope around the room for Cherry and me.

We could have stayed and watched the entertainment for a bit longer, but when

Clyde fumbled in his pocket and pulled out his own night vision goggles I thought perhaps it was time to hitch a lift on the Bernard express.

"Taxi!" I yelled.

Clyde pulled his goggles down over his eyes and looked around for us. "Smithers!" he snapped. "There they are!" He pointed at us. "Get them!"

Of course, Smithers couldn't see where Clyde was pointing. He couldn't even *tell* that Clyde was pointing. But Clyde's so self-centred he hadn't even considered bringing spare goggles for his henchboys, and the thought of giving up his own wouldn't have occurred to him. Anyway, he's afraid of the dark.

"Taxi!" I yelled again. This was our secret signal; Bernard was probably listening to us from the monster underworld, his ear pressed against the darkness beneath Sunil's bed, and he didn't want any of the other monsters hearing him being summoned by a kid. His pride's pretty fragile, really. Not to mention the fact that last time he got caught helping me, he ended up in the monster prison.

"Over here, you idiot!" Clyde raged, coming closer to us, but not too close. "Get them! Deal with them! They're here! They're right in front of meeeeeEEEE*EEEEEEE*!!!!"

The scream, of course, was because Bernard had just appeared from under the bed. Not many people are scared of him, but then not many people are like Clyde. A fact for which I am truly thankful.

"What's the matter, boss?" Smithers asked nervously.

"Ah, muh-muh-muh-muh," Clyde began. He tried again. "Muh-muh-muh-muh-muh-muh-MR BUN!!! *MR BUN!!!!!*"

Monsters live to scare people, and even Bernard is no exception. Clyde's probably the only person who's ever been scared of him, and he tends to make the most of it. He grinned, and bared his teeth. "Heh!" he chuckled. "Play time!"

"Not now, Bernard . . ." I began.

"You're right, Jack," Bernard said. "It ain't play time. It's supper time!" He opened his mouth wide. "Rrrrraaaaaarrh!" he roared, just for good measure.

Clyde squeaked and fell over.

Bernard poked him with one feathery paw. "Hmmmph," he growled. "Do you think I overdid it?"

"Boss?" Smithers asked nervously. "Boss?"

There was no reply, except for a throaty chuckle from Bernard. Smithers' nerve broke. He groped wildly in front of him, blundering around in search of the way out. Finally his hands made contact with something. It was clear from his face that he could tell straight away it wasn't the door. I think what gave it away was the fact that doors aren't usually covered in soft downy feathers.

"Hey," Bernard laughed, "that tickles!"

Smithers spun round and tried to escape; he staggered wildly across the room, fumbled his way along the wall and finally found the exit. With a terrified desperation he tugged at the handle; but Murgatroyd was still crumpled at the foot of the door, wedging it shut. Smithers gave a low moan and began to scrabble on either side.

"Come on, Bernard," I said. "Let's get out of here before he finds the switch. See you, Sunil."

"Bye, Jack," Sunil said. "Bye, Cherry. Nice to meet you, Mr Bernard."

Cherry and I dropped to our hands and knees, and followed Bernard under the bed. Within moments, the carpet was wriggling again.

The plan was to zip straight to Cherry's and talk about what little I'd learned; but it didn't work out like that. Because suddenly the nice, quiet corner of the monster underworld that Bernard was taking us through wasn't so nice and quiet after all.

One second it was just the three of us in a deserted tunnel, still on our hands and knees from crawling under Sunil's bed, the next there were thirty or forty monsters of all shapes and sizes rounding the distant

corner and bearing down on us, roaring terrifyingly.

In an instant we were on our feet. We couldn't use our torches – we'd have wiped out Bernard too – so I grabbed Freddy from my back pocket. Cherry reached into Mr Piggy and pulled out her blankie. Bernard just braced himself for the impact. The odds looked hopeless. I'd never faced so many monsters before – well, maybe once, but there was a bed in the room then.

They were almost upon us when I realized: they weren't actually looking at us. In fact, they didn't seem to have even seen us. And their roars weren't so much terrifying as terrified. They weren't running at us at all, they were running *from* something.

Bernard realized it too. He grabbed Cherry and me and shoved us against the wall, standing in front of us as a sort of monster shield. "Don't move!" he said. Then he yelped. "Ow! And put that teddy away! It stings!"

"Sorry, Bernard," I said in a muffled kind of voice. And then the monsters were stampeding past, bellowing with fear, buffeting Bernard and crushing him against us, squashing us against the hard rocky tunnel wall.

Then they were gone, disappearing round the next bend, the echoes of their panicked cries fading into the distance.

"Thanks, Bernard," I coughed, spitting

out downy monster-feathers and checking myself for bruises.

"Yeah, quick thinking," Cherry agreed. "But what's got into those things?"

"I don't know," Bernard puzzled. "It's weird, that's for sure. Monsters don't spook that easily in the monster underworld. There's nothing down here to scare us like that. Unless . . ." He stopped and shook his head, as if the thought he'd had was just too crazy even to put into words. "Naw, couldn't be."

"Unless what, Bernard?" Cherry asked. Bernard just shook his head again.

"Unless," I suggested, a bad feeling gnawing at me like a rat at a bone, "the Dark Depths are open?"

Bernard stared at me. His jaw dropped open. "Wh-what did you say?"

"Unless the Dark Depths are open," I repeated. "Is that what you were thinking?"

He nodded in sheer amazement. "How did you know?"

"Because that's what the monsters in Sunil's wardrobe told me," I said.

Bernard went pale. I'd never have believed it possible if I hadn't seen it for myself, but his soft feathery covering turned almost pure white for a moment.

"That's bad, then," Cherry guessed. "For monsters, at least."

"Not just for monsters," Bernard said, seriously worried. "The Dark Depths are where the monsters live that other monsters are scared of."

"What – monsters' monsters?" I asked. "The monsters under the monsters' beds?"

Bernard shook his head. "Not quite. Look – you know how monsters are created, right?"

Cherry and I both nodded. Bernard had explained to us before that monsters are born from the fears of children. Whatever a kid is scared of will go to make up a monster that brings those fears to life. Which is why Bernard looks like a great big bunny rabbit with downy feathers. Kids can be scared of the weirdest things.

"Well," Bernard went on, "sometimes a monster is created which is just too scary even for the monster underworld. When that happens, it's born in the Dark Depths. I don't know why; all I know is, it's always been that way."

"So where are these . . . Dark Depths then?" Cherry asked.

Bernard shrugged, and shook his head. "No one knows. All we know is, the monsters that live there can't get out – but they want to. They make noises: horrible noises that echo through the monster underworld, and can sometimes even be faintly heard coming from under the beds in your world. You won't find a monster in the underworld who isn't scared of them – even though they can't do nothing to us, 'cause they can't get out. Except . . ."

"Except, if the Dark Depths are open they *can* get out, and they *can* terrorize the monster underworld," Cherry said.

"And," I added, "they can get out from under beds as well."

We looked at each other, suddenly worried, and just for a second a flash of my dream came back to me.

"We have to close up the Dark Depths," Cherry said. "Bernard, where are they? How do we get there?"

Bernard shrugged. "I don't know," he said. "None of us ordinary monsters do. You might as well ask a human child how to get to the monster underworld."

I thought about this. "But Cherry and I *do* know how. You just follow a monster who's going there."

Cherry snapped her fingers. "Brilliant, Jack!" she said. "If we can find a monster who's going to the Dark Depths . . . but how do we do that?"

"Maybe," I suggested, "we could start by finding whatever was scaring those monsters that just ran past us."

"Which," Cherry pointed out, "means going in the direction they were coming from! Let's go!"

Bernard hesitated. "Um . . . Jack . . . Cherry . . . are you sure this is a good idea?"

"Aw, come on, Bernard!" I said. "You're not scared of a few monsters, are you? Anyway, you're with the world's greatest Monster Investigator . . ."

Cherry did that cough again.

". . . s," I added. "Investiga*tors.* We'll be fine," I went on, pleased to hear that I sounded a lot braver than I felt. "I'd like to see the monster that can get the better of me!"

Cherry kicked me, gently but threateningly, on the ankle.

"Us!" I carried on cheerfully. "The better of *us*. Come on, Bernard, we can do it."

"OK," Bernard growled. "But just make sure you keep those torches pointed away from me!"

I grinned. "Deal," I told him. "Now, let's go find that monster."

"Um, Jack," Cherry said, and for the first time ever since I'd met her she sounded just a little nervous. "I think *it's* found *us*."

I looked. Shambling round the corner in the distance was an utterly horrific figure.

And it was coming our way.

I don't know why, but it never occurred to me to doubt that this was a creature from the Dark Depths. There was something about it that made it scarier than anything I'd ever faced before.

Maybe it was because the thing looked almost human, in a horrible, warped way. It had one head, one body, two arms, two legs; but the legs were little stumpy things that ballooned out at the thighs, and the head, balanced on broad shoulders, was huge. As it got closer, I could see that the monster was wearing clothes, which was weird in itself – some kind of uniform, it looked like, with an armband. And its face was like a twisted idea of a human face, with a little twitchy moustache and a greasy hank of hair falling down over the forehead.

The eyes were quite mad.

It saw us, and stopped.

"*Ach!*" it shouted, waving one fist at us in apparent fury. Little flecks of foam sprayed from its lips. "*Shwine dass ach yabberyabber!*"

"Bernard," I said, "if things get nasty, hide and we'll use the torches."

"You know, there's something familiar about this creep," Cherry whispered.

"Another movie?" I guessed. "If your parents have been letting you watch films with creatures like that in it, then even *I* think they're being irresponsible!"

"Yeah, but not just one movie," she said, suddenly getting it. "Lots of them – and old newsreels, too! Have you done the Second World War Two in history yet?"

I shook my head. "That's next term . . . wait a minute!" Suddenly, it hit me, too. I remembered a class assembly in school about the war; a display of the class's work that term; and a book I'd once seen about a pink rabbit. "Are you saying that's . . . Hitler? The rat who started the war?

Are you saying he was a monster – I mean, a real monster – all the time?"

The creature was still frothing at the mouth, waving its fist at us, and shouting crazily.

"No," Cherry said, "but think about it. My grandad told me once that during the war lots of kids had nightmares about Hitler coming to get them . . ."

I thought about it. Thousands of children, all over Europe, scared of someone they'd only ever heard on the radio or seen in grainy photographs or newspaper cartoons, having nightmares about him, worrying about what would happen if he won the war . . .

"Of course," I said. "This isn't Hitler – it's a Hitler-monster! A monster made out of all those *fears* of Hitler . . ."

"And it's been in the Dark Depths all that time," said Bernard. "No wonder it's a bit grumpy."

A bit grumpy didn't begin to cover it. The Hitler-monster was now practically shrieking with fury, working itself up into a complete lather. Literally. Little foamy puddles of spittle were forming on the floor at its feet.

"*Fnach der bimble yung fattercatter!*" it frothed.

"So what do we do now?" Cherry wondered.

"We've got to try to get it to go back to the Dark Depths," I said.

"You think we can make it do *anything*?" Cherry asked doubtfully.

I grinned. "Why not? It's a loser. No – not even that;

it's just some worries about a loser!"

Cherry grinned back. "That's why I like you, Jack Slater," she said. "You never let a monster get the better of you. Not even one like Adolf there. Let's do it." She paused. "Only – *how* do we do it?"

"No idea," I said cheerfully. "Tell you what, let's imagine it's just a tiny little monster that we want to send back where it came from. How would you do it?"

Cherry shrugged. "Flick it with my blankie, I guess."

"Sounds like a plan," I told her, pulling Freddy out of my pocket again. "Let's give it a go. Don't slip on the foam."

The Hitler-monster saw us coming, and its mad eyes gleamed. "*Ach tuffle din dan chillybilly!*" it ranted, pounding one fist into the other hand. "*Sneggle pillarbox!*"

"What *is* it going on about?" I muttered, eyes fixed on the creature as we marched towards it.

"All part of what makes it scary," Cherry said. "Most of the kids who had nightmares about Hitler wouldn't have understood his language when they heard him on the radio. He'd have just sounded like he was shouting this kind of nonsense."

"*Finkle binkle twitbong snitmeister!*" the creature hissed furiously, beginning to stalk towards us slowly and menacingly, like some kind of predatory jungle cat. "*Arg nutter fillibonk dass monkey! Tuffle!*"

And then it rushed us. Suddenly the tunnel was a blur of high-speed monster and foamy spit. Cherry's blankie flicked out with a loud whipcrack and caught it square on the belly, but it hardly seemed to notice. A sudden tug; it ripped it out of her hand and flung it away. Then with a triumphant cry, it leaped at her.

Bernard and I were both there, one from the right and one from the left; me with Freddy the Teddy, Bernard with brute strength.

In an instant, both of us were on the floor and Freddy was sailing through the air after the blankie. Cherry was flat on her back a metre away. The monster stood over us, its face twisted in a vicious, victorious snarl, and raised its fist. "*Dass toofle shwickermuss pasta!*" it roared.

"Run!" I yelled.

We were on our feet in a flash. Cherry and I sprinted down the tunnel after Freddy and the blankie; Bernard raced in the other direction. The Hitler-monster roared again, not sure for a moment who to chase.

It chose us.

The moment's hesitation had given us a head start, and it didn't seem in a hurry, but now I knew how fast it could move when it wanted to and I wasn't going to take any chances. Cherry obviously felt the same way. Our feet slapped hard against the tunnel floor as we ran. Cherry hardly slowed as she whisked her blankie off the floor, but for some reason I fumbled Freddy and let him slip; I had to turn, twisting round on myself, almost stopping to pick him up again. As I did so I saw Bernard disappearing round the corner in the distance. He was safe; we could blast this creep without worrying. Quickly, my hand went to my torch.

It wasn't there.

I knew I'd had it a moment ago. I was sure I hadn't dropped it; but it wasn't there. There was no time to wonder what had happened to it, though; the Hitler-monster was stalking towards me, muttering insanely, eyes bright. I reached for my spare torch . . .

. . . which I'd lent to Sunil. It was safe to blast the creature, but I had nothing to blast it with.

Cherry did, though. I turned and ran.

There was no sign of Cherry in the stretch of tunnel ahead, but suddenly from round the corner came the glare of her Night Blaster 35. Its brightness thrust dazzlingly out into the tunnel in front of me and then dimmed, as if she was sweeping round like a lighthouse. Clearly she was waiting for me – and lying in wait for the

monster. *Good plan, Cherry!* I thought. If it followed me round the bend, it'd get blasted out of existence – but maybe it wouldn't dare. In which case, perhaps we could herd it back to where it had come from, and find out where the Dark Depths were.

All that went through my head as I made for the bend, legs pumping like pumps that couldn't keep pumping much longer. Now I was only seconds away; but it sounded like the Hitler-monster was only seconds behind me. I didn't look round; I kept running, racing for that corner.

I was there. With a gasp of relief, I swung round the bend. "Quick . . ." I gasped. "It's right be—"

The sentence dried up in my mouth as my eyes took in the scene. The Night Blaster was lying as if it had been dropped, its bright beam pointed at the wall. Beside it lay the crumpled blankie.

Cherry was nowhere to be seen.

My heart sank; but there was no time to think about what might have happened to Cherry. The sound of danger came from behind me. I whirled.

"*Snickersnacker!*" hissed the Hitler-monster, advancing menacingly. Its bloodshot eyes gleamed hungrily; its claw-like hands reached out eagerly for me.

I snatched up the Night Blaster and blasted it.

Nothing happened.

Actually, plenty happened, but the one thing that *should* have happened, didn't. It didn't vanish.

What it did do was roar furiously, and leap at me, lashing out angrily. I skidded backwards, holding the dazzling beam full in its face out of instinct more than anything. I didn't know what else to do. My mind scrabbled for ideas, but all I could think was: monsters are supposed to vanish

when you shine a torch at them! What do you do when a monster breaks the rules? Tell a teacher? Write an angry letter to someone?

It leaped again; I skidded backwards once more – and found myself up against the wall. There was a kink in the tunnel I hadn't noticed, and now I had nowhere left to go. Desperately, I kept the Night Blaster's huge reflector trained on the insane, angry monster; but to no avail.

"*Dorf du sandvitch chickenuggets!*" it shrieked, spraying foam like an irate fire extinguisher, and raked at my face with its hands. I ducked, too late.

For a moment I wondered why it didn't hurt. Then it lashed out again, and this time I saw its hands pass right through me and on into the tunnel wall.

"*Nik tuffle deng cracklybitz!*" it screamed, striking me once more; and once more its hands just passed through me harmlessly.

Now it noticed it too. Its eyes widened in puzzlement. "*Pigsnuggler!*" it exclaimed, stepping back; and I noticed that it looked somehow different. It took me a moment to realize that, very faintly, the tunnel wall was showing through it. Not before time, it was slowly beginning to disappear.

I raised the Night Blaster and shone it right in its face.

It reared up and slashed at me again and again, but it was clearly fading now, turning more and more transparent with every passing second. "*Footinbooten!*" it stormed. "*Chattanooga!*" The tunnel wall was becoming visible through its ever more ghostly form. It raged and ranted in its strange gibberish as it flailed uselessly at me, but even its voice was beginning to fade away. "*Buttervagon der tinklebuster slopphouse!*" it seethed hoarsely. "*Ick yabberyabber das rickenbacker vaxverk!*" it continued, its voice now coming as if from far away; and then,

just as it winked out of existence altogether, it added weakly, "Oh, *bum*!"

Shakily, I switched off the Night Blaster and wiped the foam from the front of my sweatshirt. If the Hitler-monster was typical of the creatures from the Dark Depths, I could see why the other monsters were so scared of them. That had been the toughest fight of my career, by a long way.

And my troubles weren't over yet. Cherry had vanished – taken, at a guess, by something else from the Dark Depths.

I wondered if all of them were as resistant to light and to snugglies as Adolf had been. And if so, what could I do against them? How could I rescue her? Suddenly exhausted, I leaned against the tunnel wall and shook my head in despair.

That was when a voice spoke from out of the darkness.

"Ready to give in yet, Jack Slater?" it whispered.

I raised the Night Blaster. "Who's there?" My night vision goggles seemed to be working perfectly, but there was no sign of anyone – or any*thing* – near me in the tunnel.

The voice chuckled softly. "Me, Jack? I'm your worst nightmare."

"Actually," I said, my finger tightening on the switch, my eyes searching the darkness, "my worst nightmare was the one about standing up in assembly with no pants on. I guess that makes you the

No-Pants Monster."

"More like the No-*Chance* Monster," it hissed. "No chance for you, that is. You might as well give up now."

"I don't do giving up," I told it, still trying to work out where the voice was coming from. "You're talking to the world's greatest Monster Investigator. I'd like to see the monster that can get the better of me."

It chuckled again, a sound like warm fat glugging slowly down a plughole. "You will, Jack. You will. Just find your way to the Dark Depths and try to rescue your friends. Then you'll see the monster who can beat you. The monster who *will* beat you. The monster who *has* beaten you."

"*Has* beaten me?" I scoffed. "No monster's ever beaten me."

"Really?" the voice said. "Then tell me, Jack – where's your torch?"

Instinctively, though I already knew the torch was missing, my hand went to my pocket again. The monster saw the movement, and laughed softly. "It's not there, is it, Jack? Because I took it from you, and you never even noticed. Face it, Jack – I'm too smart for you, too fast for you, too cunning for you. I've got your torch; I've got your friends; I've got it all worked out. You've got no chance against me."

"Is that so?" I said. "Why all this hiding in the shadows then? Too scared even to tell me who you are? Face me like a monster and we'll see who's got no chance."

That soft chuckle came again. It was really starting to get on my nerves. "If you need a name, you can call me Mr Whisper.

And as for facing me – you'll get your chance. I'll see you in the Dark Depths."

"Which are where, exactly?" I asked. "I left my *A to Z* of the monster underworld at home."

"The nose knows, Jack," Mr Whisper teased, sounding irritatingly pleased with himself. "Just follow the nose."

"Right, very helpful," I said. "You mean I've got to find you by smell? Or I've got to go straight ahead? What do you mean, follow the nose?"

There was no answer.

"I've got to guess, do I?" I asked.

Still there was no answer. The mysterious Mr Whisper, it seemed, had gone. And I had a huge problem.

From what the monster had said – twice

– about having my friends, I had to assume that Bernard as well as Cherry had been captured. Which meant I was on my own.

And on my own I had to find the Dark Depths, defeat a monster who could sneak my torch from my pocket without my noticing and against whom my weapons were probably useless, and rescue Cherry and Bernard.

For perhaps the first time since I became a Monster Investigator, I was really, properly, genuinely scared.

I had no idea what Mr Whisper had meant by "follow the nose".

What made it worse was that there was another little voice whispering away in the back of my head, telling me I didn't stand a chance. "*Might as well give up*," it was saying. "*You'll never find them. There's no point. You'll end up wandering around here for ever.*"

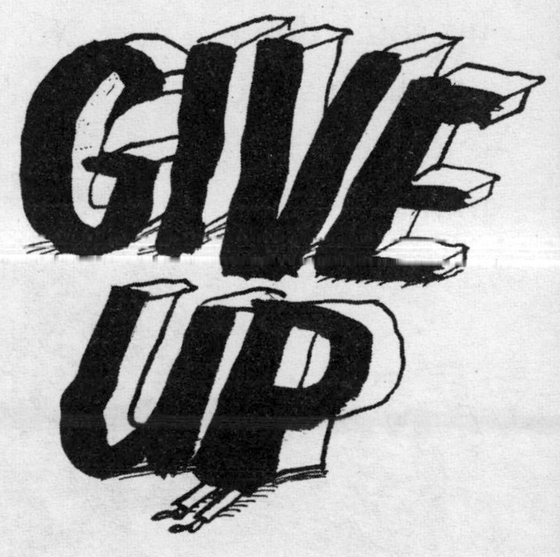

I gritted my teeth and ignored it. My friends needed me.

Picking up Cherry's blankie, I folded it carefully and slipped it into my backpack. Then, Night Blaster at the ready, I set off back the way I'd come, hoping that if I could find the Hitler-monster's trail it would lead me to the Dark Depths.

For quite some time, it was easy. There were no junctions; no forks; there was nowhere to go wrong. But after a while I found myself faced with an impossible choice. The tunnel widened, branching out into five separate paths, two of which split into more almost immediately. Some sloped up, some down. There was no way of telling which one the Hitler-monster had

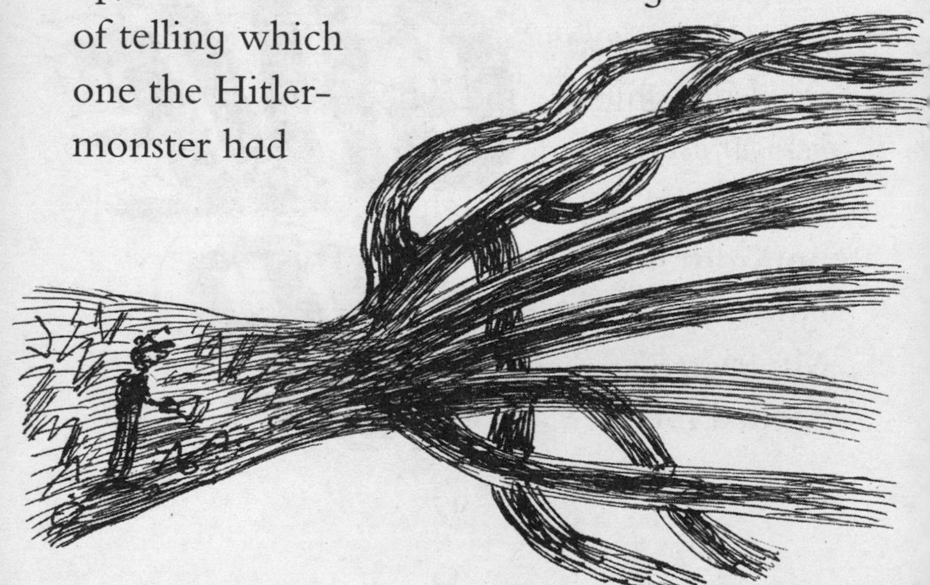

come from. I followed each of them for a few metres, looking for clues, but there was nothing. In the back of my mind, the little voice – the voice of my own fears – was more insistent now, telling me that no one would blame me if I gave up now.

But *I* would have blamed me. So I kept on looking; and before long I noticed something. A little way down one of the tunnels, just where it split into three more, there were a lot of tiny pieces of crumbled rock all over the ground. I looked up and noticed something I'd missed before. The three new tunnels were lower than the one I was standing in, and where the ceiling sloped down towards them, someone – or something – had scratched some kind of markings into the rock face. They were words – difficult to read not just because they weren't very deep, but also because monsters as a rule don't have much in the way of literacy skills. Eventually, though, after much peering, I was able to work out what they said:

Keep owt! Privut. No monsters frum the Dark Depths. No bigg shiney briyt scary liyts. No horrid litul monstrinvestigatrs. No thru rode.

Now, if I hadn't seen this, I'd probably have headed back the way I'd come and tried to think of something else. But you know how it is – someone tells you you can't do something you hadn't even thought of doing, and suddenly it seems like a great idea. Besides which, it looked as if maybe someone had something to hide.

The words stretched, more or less, across all three tunnels. So the question was: which one to pick? I stood, scratching my head for a moment, before the answer came to me. What was it Mr Whisper had said?

"*The nose knows, Jack. Just follow the nose.*"

I looked up again. The word "NO" appeared four times in the unevenly written message; and all four lined up, more or less, over the entrance to the middle tunnel – almost as if they were pointing at it.

"*Follow the nose.*"

What if he'd meant: "*Follow the 'no's*"?

"Follow the 'no's," I said to myself as, Night Blaster at the ready, I stepped forward into the tunnel. "Of course – the 'n-o's, not the 'n-o-s-e'."

And that, of course, was when the biggest nose in the world jumped out and sniffed me up inside it.

My first instinct was to panic, which would have been a bad idea. My second was to take a deep breath to calm myself down. That would have been a worse idea; the inside of the nose was horribly hairy and sticky, and I don't even want to think what I might have sucked in.

My third instinct was to switch on the Night Blaster, which I was still gripping firmly; but something told me not to. If this nose could lead me to the Dark

Depths, I didn't want it disappearing in a blaze of torchlight – not if I could avoid it.

So I went with instinct number four. With difficulty – there wasn't much room to move – I eased Freddy the Teddy out of my pocket and rubbed him, hard, against the inside of the giant nostril.

AAAAAAAAAACHOOO!!!

The tremendous sneeze threw me out and down, hard, while the recoil shot the nose up in the air and across the tunnel. It rebounded from the wall and crashed to the floor. Dripping with something I'd rather not talk about, I leaped to my feet and pointed the Night Blaster threateningly.

"Don't try anything!" I growled.

"Hey! Easy, kid!" came a voice, and for a moment I wondered what a nose could possibly use to speak with. Then I realized that three of the legs underneath the nose didn't belong to it. It struggled to its own feet – two small ones on spindly limbs at the back – and stepped cautiously to one side, revealing the monster it had fallen on. It was a little puffball of a creature, almost completely round except for three legs underneath and two arms that stuck out from the side of its head. Or maybe it was its body. Whichever it was, it was covered in spiky fur through which two round eyes gleamed.

"We ain't going to hurt you!" Puffball went on, clambering to its feet.

"You could have fooled me," I retorted. "Being sniffed up inside Sneezy there isn't exactly my idea of fun."

"Yeah, but we was just doing what we was told!" Puffball said pleadingly, eyeing the Night Blaster nervously. The nose sniffed in agreement. "We's supposed to take you to—"

"The Dark Depths?" I suggested. They both nodded. Well, the nose just kind of bobbed up and down a bit, which I expect

is the best it could do.

"So why don't you let Augustus sniff you up again like the boss said, and we'll take you?" Puffball went on.

"No way," I said. "It tickles in there. And just to check – "the boss" means . . . ?"

The little spiky monster looked left and right, as if nervous of being heard. "Mr Whisper," it muttered darkly. The nose, Augustus, shivered. "Aw, c'mon, kid," Puffball begged; and then its eyes took on a crafty look and its voice hardened. "You wanna see your friends again, you better get in the nose right now, yeah?"

I gave it the eyeball right back. "If you want to have to go back and tell Mr Whisper that you failed to do what he told you to, you're going the right way about it!"

Augustus quivered again, and just for an instant Puffball's spiky fur paled. "Aw . . . come on!" it said again, its voice trembling a little. "You . . . you *got* to come with us!"

"*With* you, maybe," I said. "Inside you – no. Lead the way, and no funny business."

Puffball shook its head. Or body; I still wasn't sure. "It's a long way," it said, "and we're two of the fastest monsters down here. That's why Mr Whisper . . . um . . . recruited us." There was something in the way it said this that made me think they hadn't been entirely willing volunteers. "You'd never keep up," it went on. "You can't reach the Dark Depths if you ain't in the nose. There just ain't no other way."

"There's always another way," I said.

Fortunately, Augustus was what they call a Roman nose – one of those great big hooked hooters with a little, almost flat bit that sticks straight out from between the eyes. Or would have done if it'd been attached to a face. It didn't make a perfect saddle – it was a bit slippy, for one thing – but after a couple of hard landings I learned how to grip with my knees, and then we were off.

Puffball was right – I'd never have kept up. The monster underworld turned into one long blur as Augustus accelerated to a gallop and beyond. Boy, could that nose run.

The best thing about going so quickly, talking about noses running, was that it helped me to dry out. It wasn't long before I was able to brush off most of what my brief stay in Augustus's nostril had left on my hair and clothes, leaving a little crispy trail littering the tunnels behind us.

On we raced, my legs starting to ache with the effort of holding on so tightly, until eventually we hit a long, straight tunnel that seemed to stretch on for miles. Augustus accelerated.

As the nose ran faster, I peered ahead of

us. Soon I could make out a hard, rocky wall at the end of the corridor, in the distance but coming rapidly nearer. I hoped Augustus's brakes were in good working order.

The wall drew closer. It looked to me as if this was where the tunnel stopped; there was no sign of a curve or a corner.

"Um, Augustus," I said, "maybe you might want to think about slowing down?"

There was no answer, except perhaps a slight increase in speed. I began to feel a little nervous.

"Have you ever seen what happens when a nose hits a wall?" I asked, my eyes on the approaching obstruction. "It's not pretty. They get all bent out of shape; there's blood everywhere . . . Augustus, *I really think you might want to slow down*!"

Augustus made a snorting sound and raced on. And now the wall was rushing towards us, big and hard and jagged. There was no way of stopping in time. And at this speed, jumping off would be deadly.

I was trapped – with no way of escape – on top of a suicidal nose, about to be smashed against sheer craggy rock.

I barely had time to hope that Augustus would take most of the impact before the wall was upon us. I braced for collision.

The rocky surface rippled as we entered it.

Moving through the wall was a bit like wading through honey. By the time we emerged on the other side we'd slowed down almost to walking speed and, as soon as we were through, Augustus stopped. I slid off and peered into the darkness.

Yes, I know the whole of the monster underworld is in darkness, but this was a darker darkness, if that makes any sense. My night vision goggles were still working, but somehow everything seemed gloomier

than before; and even though there was no light, there were shadows.

"So these are the Dark Depths," I murmured, turning just in time to see the rocky wall rippling once more as Puffball pushed through to join us. "You didn't think of warning me we were going to run through a rock at a hundred miles an hour, then?"

Puffball shrugged – not an easy feat for someone with no shoulders. "We're monsters. You think we're gonna pass up an opportunity to scare a kid?"

I shrugged back, and put my hand on the rock we'd just walked through. It was completely solid.

"All the doors into the Dark Depths are one-way," Puffball told me. "Ain't nothing can get out."

"Except that monsters are getting out," I reminded him. "And what about you two? Are you telling me you're stuck here now?"

"Naw," Puffball said. "The boss can open the doors from this side – just for a second at a time; just long enough to let one monster out into the underworld, or maybe two, if they're quick, but—"

Augustus sniffed disapprovingly and Puffball broke off suddenly, as if it'd been caught talking about something it shouldn't. Just as quickly, it changed the subject, gabbling in an attempt to distract me.

"Course, Augustus and me, we ain't from the Dark Depths ourselves. We only work here – just since yesterday, that's all. We just follow the boss's orders. 'Get the kid,' he says, so we get the kid. Between you and me, I wouldn't do it if I didn't have to. I'm just an ordinary everyday monster under the bed. Scaring kids, that's what we do. Show me a kid, I'll scare him. Boo! Just like that, see? I'm happy with all o' that side of things. It's this other stuff I'm not sure about . . ."

Augustus sniffed again, louder, and Puffball clammed up again. But a thought had just occurred to me.

"I'm not the first kid you've brought here this evening, am I?" I asked suspiciously. "Did you two snatch a girl from the tunnels earlier? About my height, with beads in her hair, carrying a piggy backpack and wearing—"

"I can't say nothing more," Puffball interrupted. It seemed a little subdued all of a sudden. "I've said too much already. The boss gets to hear about it, I'm done for."

Augustus bobbed up and down, nodding. It sniffed loudly.

"Yeah, you're right, Gus," Puffball said. "Sorry about this, fella – you seem like a nice enough kid, even if you don't scream an' all; but the boss is waiting for you. It's this way. Let's go."

I felt pretty subdued myself as we set off in the direction Puffball had indicated. There was no wriggling carpet underfoot; our footsteps echoed ominously in the wide stony passageway. Down the tunnel sloped, deeper into the Dark Depths, and all the while I was thinking about Mr Whisper. What if he was right? What if I *had* finally met my match? What if there was no way of beating him? I shivered and pushed these treacherous thoughts away, but they kept crowding back again like kids round an ice-cream van, greedy for my attention.

Presently, we came to a door that blocked the tunnel. Augustus and Puffball came to a stop in front of it.

"This is it, kid," Puffball said. "Through the door. The boss'll be . . . waiting for you. For what it's worth, I'm sorry we had to bring you here. It's been nice knowing you."

"You're just trying to scare me," I said, trying to unscare myself.

Puffball shook its head – or body, or whatever. "Wish I was. *Scaring* kids is fine; it's what monsters are for. But—" It broke off. Augustus sniffed; but this time it sounded more sad than anything else.

"Yeah, well," I said, sounding a whole lot braver than I felt. "Thanks for getting me here. But you guys better not turn up under any beds I'm protecting, or there'll be trouble." I winked at them. They smiled back. Don't ask me how I know that, since neither of them had anything visible in the way of mouths, but take it from me, they smiled. They weren't such bad guys, for monsters. "Come on, let's go."

Puffball shook its whatever again. "The boss told us to bring you here and show you the way in. We ain't going no further." It shuddered. "It's scary in there."

I almost shuddered myself. Now that I was this close to meeting Mr Whisper face to face, I was feeling pretty freaked out. I took a deep breath and thought of Cherry and Bernard. There are times when a Monster Investigator's got to do what a Monster Investigator's got to do, and this was one of those times.

With one more nod at Puffball and Augustus I opened the door and stepped through, reaching into my backpack for the Night Blaster. Ahead of me was another length of tunnel, but with a difference: the walls were smooth and straight, and the floor flat and even. Behind me the door slammed shut as, squaring my shoulders, I walked towards the archway at the end of the corridor and into the largest cavern I had ever seen.

Really, it was immense. Absolutely enormous.

And so was the machine that filled the middle of the chamber, dwarfing all the monsters in overalls that were busily hurrying to and fro on the surrounding walkways. It towered high over us, emitting a gently threatening hum, like one of those doomsday weapons that mad scientists in spy movies are always inventing. All it needed was for some criminal mastermind to step out of the shadows and tell me how he was going to use it to take over the world. Something about it horrified me; all my instincts were yelling at me to run while I had the chance.

I didn't get to be the world's greatest

Monster Investigator by not listening to my instincts – but I didn't get there by running away, either. As quietly as I could I stepped forward, Night Blaster at the ready.

An enormous paw seized my arm. I wheeled round, raising the Night Blaster, but suddenly it was snatched out of my hand, and that, too, was caught and held. Two huge hairy monsters had stepped silently out of the shadows and grabbed me. My heart jolted for a moment, and I mentally kicked myself for letting them take me by surprise. My feet scraping the

ground, I was dragged forwards towards the gigantic device.

As we approached, I could see a lone figure standing at the base of the machine. It didn't look terribly scary – in fact, from a distance it looked almost human – yet there was something chilling about it. I felt myself go numb with fear. This had to be the monster who'd captured my friends; the monster who had promised to face me and beat me here in the Dark Depths.

Mr Whisper.

He was standing with his back to us, his bald, scaly, bullet-shaped head looking up at the machine. Where his neck should have been, his head disappeared into the collar of what looked like a very sharp suit. He turned as we neared him; in his arms he held what could have been a fluffy white cat, except that it had a tail at each end and its face in the middle of its body. There was something snake-like about the way he stroked it. His reptilian eyes gleamed darkly as they fixed on me, and his lipless mouth stretched into a chilling grin.

"Ah, Mr Slater," he said. "I've been expecting you."

"This is what you call facing me like a monster, is it, Whisper?" I raged, struggling in vain against the two huge hairies who held me.

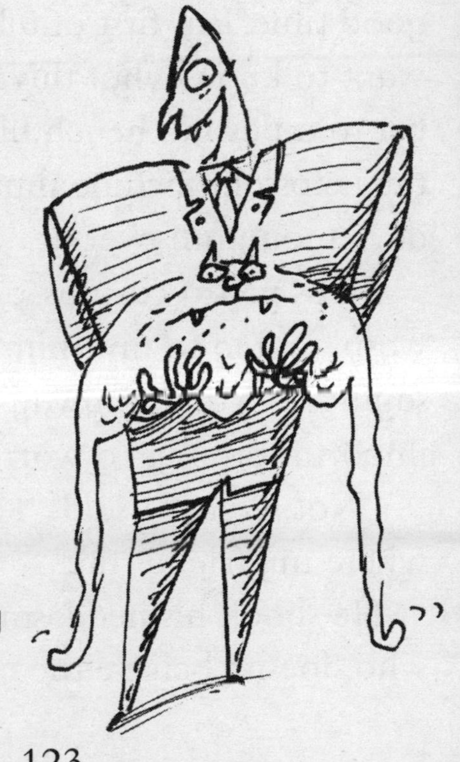

Whisper's grin stretched even wider. "Why, yes, Jack, it is. You don't expect a monster to play fair, do you?"

I supposed he had a point. It was no big surprise to be captured, in any case. Whisper had known I was coming, and he'd set it up so there'd been no way to avoid walking into his trap – except by not coming at all, and I reckoned he'd known I wouldn't do that. It felt like he'd been ahead of me every step of the way. I began to wonder if he ever made a mistake.

"Where are my friends?" I demanded.

"All in good time," he told me. "All in good time. But first of all, I suppose you want to know what this is?" Handing his pet to a passing henchthing, he indicated the colossal machine that loomed like a dark mountain over us.

I was pretty curious, actually, but I wasn't going to give him the satisfaction of saying so – and anyway, there were more important things to worry about.

"Not really," I said. "I'd rather know where my friends are."

He shook his head, smiling like a teacher who doesn't believe the cat ate your homework but can't be bothered to get cross about it. "I think you'll change your mind in a minute. But perhaps your friends would be interested in hearing this, too." He nodded to the Hairy Twins. "Fetch Mr Slater's friends. Oh, and put his weapons somewhere safe. He'll behave himself – won't you, Jack?"

I scowled at him as the hairies reluctantly let go and moved off, taking both my torch and my backpack with them. He was right – again. There was nothing I could do; I was unarmed, there were monsters everywhere, and I had no idea how strong Whisper himself was. I folded my arms and glared at him.

He smiled a humourless smile. "That's a good boy.

There's no point in making a fuss, is there? You can't beat me, you know. I really am much too clever for you."

I kept on glaring, but inside I felt colder than a polar bear's toes. No monster had ever scared me like Mr Whisper did. The worst thing of all was – he was right. He *was* too clever for me. I felt suddenly sure that he'd planned all this – scaring those monsters into Sunil's wardrobe so that we'd go to his house; watching how we got there so he'd know which way we'd come back; setting the Hitler-monster on us to stop us from returning home; separating us from each other; capturing Cherry and Bernard so that I'd have to come looking for them. Now he'd got me, too. This was a monster who got nothing wrong. And a monster who got nothing wrong was a monster who couldn't be beaten.

"Your friends are here, Jack," Whisper said softly.

I turned – and my heart, which had been sinking slowly into a deep pit of despair, suddenly bobbed right back up again with a happy smile on its face. Because it wasn't Cherry and Bernard who were being escorted towards us by the Shaggy Brothers.

It was Cherry and Clyde.

And this made me very happy on two counts. Firstly, because it meant Bernard was still out there somewhere, which meant in turn that there was still a hope, however faint, of rescue.

And secondly, and much more importantly: if Mr Whisper thought it was in any way sensible, reasonable, or even slightly not-at-all-completely-bonkers to even begin to think about possibly perhaps describing Clyde Pumfrey-Soames as my friend, then he wasn't as smart as he thought he was. He'd just shown me he *could* make mistakes. And maybe, just maybe, that meant he could be beaten after all.

"Hey, Jack," Cherry said, managing to flash me a brave grin despite everything. Not for the first time, I was proud to be her partner.

"Hi," I returned. "You OK?"

She nodded. "I'm fine. Bit bored, though. They don't even have TV down here."

"Slater!" Clyde sniffled in a weepy sort of voice. "This is all your fault! Get me out of here!"

There was something odd about the way he was looking around, almost as if he couldn't see properly; for a moment I couldn't work out what was the matter. Then he flipped up his night-vision lenses. Water flooded out of them and streamed down the front of his shirt. Clearly Clyde had forgotten one of the first rules of monster investigating: never cry inside your goggles. He sniffed again, and turned to Mr Whisper. "You've got what you want now. You don't need me. Why don't you let me go?"

Whisper ignored him. "Now, Jack," he said, "time for me to explain everything to you."

"You know," said Cherry, "I had a feeling you were going to do just that. This is going to be something about taking over the world, isn't it?"

Whisper smiled again, like a python that's eaten something amusing. "Clever girl," he purred. "But why don't you let me tell the story my way?" He cocked one scaly eyebrow at her and, after a moment, continued. "I was born here in the Dark Depths, Jack. It's where all the worst of us are born, and it's where we stay. The barriers that separate us from the monster underworld are one-way – you can get in, but you can't get out. No monster has ever escaped from the Dark Depths.

"But then, no monster has ever been such a genius as me. I knew there must be a way to force the barriers open, if only I could find it – and, after years of trying, I did." His snake-eyes narrowed into little black dots. "You can't imagine it, Jack. The sense of freedom after a lifetime's captivity! I squeezed through the barriers and made my way out into the monster underworld, terrifying the feeble little excuses for monsters I found there.

"But after only a few minutes," he went

on, his voice dropping to a hiss, "I found myself drawn back here by a force I could not resist. It was as if the Dark Depths was a magnet, and I was an iron filing. Try as I might, I could not escape for more than fifteen minutes at a time! And neither could the other monsters I released from this dark prison."

He paused for effect.

Cherry butted right in. "So you swore you were going to get revenge on the world, and you built this big mean machine, right?"

Whisper glared fiercely at her.

"Hey, don't look so surprised," Cherry went on. "I've lost count of the movies I've seen where the bad guy's got a sob story like that. Just get to the point and tell us what the evil master plan is, so we can defeat you and go home, OK?"

Mr Whisper hissed softly. Clyde whimpered like a baby and tried to hide.

"Very well, Miss Jackson," Whisper said. "The evil master plan, as you call it, is quite simple. As for the 'mean machine', I prefer

to think of it as my Depth Charge – or, if you prefer, my Dark Depths Charge." He chuckled coldly, as if he'd said something funny. "Once it is powered up, it will generate a shock wave that will shatter the barriers that hold us here. All the monsters that have been trapped in the Dark Depths will be released into the monster underworld."

"Until they're dragged back like iron filings," I pointed out. "They'll only be out scaring the other monsters for fifteen minutes. It could be worse."

"Oh, it will be, Jack. *Much* worse." Whisper smiled again. I hated it when he did that. "You see, once the last monster has departed, my Depth Charge will explode. The Dark Depths will be utterly destroyed. There will be nothing left to drag us back. The most terrifying monsters that ever existed will be free to roam not only the monster underworld, but also the world of humans. None of you will be safe! Your armies and your police forces will be powerless against us! And then I—"

"Will rule the world!" Cherry cut in again. "You've watched those movies a lot of times, haven't you? How'd you manage that, seeing as you don't have television down here and you can only get out for fifteen minutes at a time?"

"I checked the programme guides and just came out to watch the best bits," Whisper hissed impatiently. "And now," he went on, "it's time to put my evil master plan into action!"

A movement caught my eye. Three monsters had entered the chamber through a nearby door, each pushing – of all things – a bed. A Pumfrey-Soames skatebed, to be precise – the bed on wheels that was Clyde's dad's furniture company's biggest seller. I had no idea what Whisper's goons wanted with them – but maybe, just maybe, they could help us. I looked at Cherry and Clyde; they'd noticed them too. Now I could only hope they'd realize what I was doing and follow my lead.

"One!" I said, stepping forward. The old counting-to-five-as-you-get-into-bed routine had never failed me yet.

"One!" Cherry counted behind me, and a moment later I heard Clyde's voice tremble, "One!"

The hairies looked at Whisper. He shrugged. "There's a bed in the room, gentlemen," he said. "You know the rules."

"Two!" we chorused, my heart filling up with hope like a fat kid fills up at McDonald's. I'd been taking a chance – I didn't know whether the counting-to-five manoeuvre would work against monsters from the Dark Depths. It was good to know it did.

If I hadn't been so nervous, I might have stopped to wonder why Whisper didn't look at all concerned, and why he needed three skatebeds in the first place. But I was so focused on getting us to the beds by five that it didn't occur to me.

"Three!" We reached the beds and hopped onto them. "Four!" we went on, snuggling down under the covers. "Five!" we finished, just because you have to finish the count or it doesn't, um, count.

"Well done, Jack!" Mr Whisper hissed. "You reached the beds by five, and now we can't touch you. You seem to have forgotten something, though."

"What's that, Whisper?" I asked cheerily – more cheerily than I felt, anyway.

He squatted down by the bed and looked at me. "You've forgotten, Jack, that I'm much, much smarter than you are." He took from his suit pocket some kind of remote control and pressed a button.

Click! In an instant hidden straps shot out from under the bed frame, looped over me and tightened with a loud snapping noise around the duvet, pinning my arms to

my sides. Straining, I twisted my head to see Cherry and Clyde trapped in just the same way.

"You see, Jack," Whisper went on triumphantly, "all I need to power my machine – my Depth Charge – is fear." He bent closer, and his voice dropped to a cold whisper. "*Your* fear."

I was trembling as the monsters pushed us back towards the door they'd come through.

Which meant I was doing a lot better than Clyde, who was crying like a baby. If Whisper's machine ran on fear, he could just have plugged Clyde straight into it. He'd probably have had enough energy left over to make every monster in the Dark Depths

a cup of tea and keep it warm until Christmas.

Except that Whisper hadn't just said he needed fear to power his Depth Charge. He'd said he needed *my* fear. And I couldn't see why. What was so special about my fear? Apart from the fact that it was normally in short supply, of course. I wished there was less of it just now.

Whisper led the way through the door and into a large room – nowhere near as large as the vast chamber that housed the Depth Charge, but a lot bigger than the average bedroom, with much higher ceilings. As best I could from where I lay strapped to the skatebed, I strained to take a look around.

The first thing I noticed was a wide ramp that sloped up to the height of a tall wall that stretched right across the middle of the room. There were some unpleasantly squelchy noises coming from behind the wall. Three bungees were attached at one end to the top of the ramp. They dangled down like tree snakes, with huge heavy padlocks where their heads should be. To the wall opposite the ramp were fixed three fairly thin and weedy-looking ropes, with the same sort of padlocks hanging down from their free ends. Something told me this was Not A Good Thing.

The only crumb of comfort was that all of our stuff – backpacks, torches, Freddy the Teddy, Cherry's blankie – were piled up in the corner. As comforts go, though, that one really was pretty crumby. We had no way of getting to them.

The monsters wheeled us over to the ropes and clamped them onto the frames of the skatebeds, just behind our heads. Then they scurried up the ramp to grab the bungees, which they st-r-e-tch-ed with all their might until they were close enough to padlock them to the feet of the beds.

That done, they scurried from the chamber as fast as they could, leaving us alone with Mr Whisper.

Whisper squatted down beside me. "So, Jack," he said, "you'll want to know what all this is for, won't you?"

A witty retort sprang to my lips. Unfortunately, my lips were so dry with fear that they stuck together, trapping the witty retort inside. Luckily, Cherry was still there.

"We know what this is about," she said. "This is about you planning some ridiculously complicated way to get rid of us."

Whisper's smile stretched like a bungee. "Well, of course. But it's also about generating enough fear inside young

Master Slater here to power my Depth Charge – twice. You see, the walls of this room are lined with fear receptors, which will pick up his fear and carry it to the control panel. The more frightened he gets, the more power will build up. And believe me, Jack," he went on, "you've never been as frightened before as you're *going* to be, now, in here. You see this wall? Behind it lurk some quite terrifying monsters. And they're hungry, Jack – very hungry.

"You're a bright boy, of course – not as bright as me, but then, who is? I'm sure, though, that you're bright enough to have worked out the rest. However, as your friend Miss Jackson will agree, it's traditional that I, as the master villain, spell it out for you." He pointed towards my feet. "The only thing stopping the bungees at that end of the bed from twanging you over the wall and into the waiting arms – or paws, or claws, or tentacles – of the monsters on the other side, is the rope at this end of the bed."

He plucked the now tightly stretched rope; it vibrated with a deep thrumming noise that reverberated through the bed frame.

"But what if the rope snapped?" He grinned unpleasantly. "Let's find out, shall we?" He took from his pocket a matchbox. It was shaking and making little squeaking sounds. "You may have noticed that the rope smells a little . . . cheesy. That's deliberate; it's to make it oh-so-tempting for these little fellows." He gave the matchbox a pat. "I understand you've met the Prime Minister? It may interest you to know that in his younger days he had rather stinky feet. And he had nightmares about little creatures that would come and nibble his toes, all the while saying, 'Mmmm! Cheese! Gorgonzola! Stilton!' You know how monsters are created, don't you, Jack? They're made from the fears of children – even children who may grow up to become Prime Minister. Jack Slater and friends, may I introduce to you – the cheesy toe nibblers!"

He sauntered over to Clyde's bed. Clyde whimpered in terror as Mr Whisper slowly pushed open the matchbox, and the first of the cheesy toe nibblers scampered out.

They were like tiny little mice, with big sharp teeth that set to work on the rope straight away.

"It'll take them a few minutes to gnaw through the ropes, of course – just time for you to get really, really frightened," Whisper went on, as he strolled over to Cherry and shook a few more cheesy toe nibblers out onto the rope that held her skatebed. "And when the rope snaps – *twang!* Up the ramp you'll go, faster and faster, hurtling towards certain doom. The straps that hold you and your friends to the beds will release automatically, and over the wall you'll go." His smile widened, showing a mouthful of big, square teeth. "Do you like the wall, Jack? I had it built specially, and behind it I've put some of the most horrifying monsters I could find. Just for

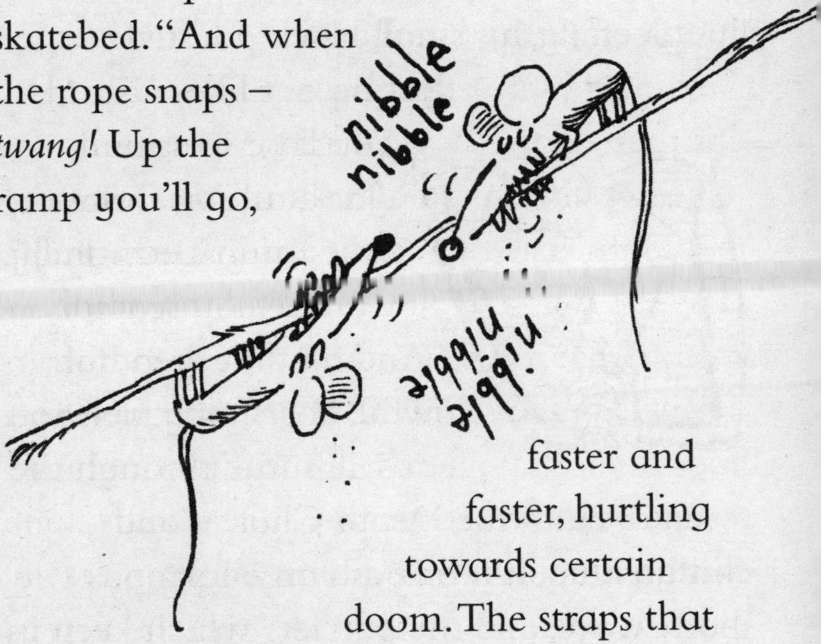

you. They're going to have such fun when you and your friends join them on the other side. But you won't." He licked his lips gleefully, his small black pointed tongue darting out like a lizard. "You'll be so scared, Jack, as you shoot up the ramp. Beautifully, wonderfully scared. And all that dreadful, awful, horrifying, delicious fear will surge through the receptors into the Depth Charge and charge it up. It'll unleash an enormous shock wave, and the barriers which keep us here will be blasted open. Wide open. And they'll stay open long enough for all the monsters from the Dark Depths to be released into the monster underworld!"

He wandered over to my rope and sprinkled the last few cheesy toe eaters onto it. "Yum!" they squeaked. "Cheesy Cheddar!

Camembert! Parmesan!" Their little teeth went *snick! snick! snick!* as they set to work.

"But of course," Mr Whisper went on, "there's no point in releasing my fellow monsters if the Dark Depths are just going to drag them back fifteen minutes later, is there? Which is where the second part of my evil master plan, as Miss Jackson calls it, comes in. You see, Jack, the Depth Charge won't just use your fear to blast away the barriers. Not at all." He grinned nastily. "Once you get over that wall, you'll see exactly what kind of monsters are waiting for you – and then you'll get *really* scared! For the second time, your fear will power up the Depth Charge. And this time, when it's fully charged and all the monsters have been released, I shall set the timer, make my escape, and then – BOOM! – one huge explosion, and no more Dark Depths.

"And no more Jack Slater to bother us as

we take over the human world, either. I'm going to enjoy it so much, Jack. My only regret is that I can't stay around to watch you going over the wall. But someone's got to operate the control panel, and I'm the only one whose hands are the right shape. Besides – as Miss Jackson will tell you, it's traditional."

"Oh, yeah?" Cherry spat at him as he left. "Well, it's also traditional that the hero gets out of the trap and beats the bad guy before the end credits!"

But Mr Whisper had gone, and there was no answer.

The clock was ticking.

Actually, that's just a figure of speech – there was no clock in the room. But the *snick-snick-snick* of the cheesy toe nibblers' teeth was like a countdown to doom.

And the 'Eeeeeee! Eeeeeeeeeeeeeeeee!' noise that Clyde was making was like an annoying kid making a really annoying noise in the most annoying way possible. Between the *snick*s and the *eeeeeee*s, it was hard to think.

"Shut *up*, Clyde," I growled for about the hundredth time.

Clyde ignored me. "Eeeeeeee!" he said.

"What do we do, Cherry?" I asked. "Any ideas?"

"Uh-uh," she answered. "You ever been in a fix as bad as this one?"

"Only once," I said.

She perked up. "Really? How'd you get out of it?"

"You popped out from under the bed and rescued me," I told her.

"Oh." She paused. "I don't think I can do that this time. Any other ideas?"

"Nope," I said, craning my head to check out the damage to the rope. The toe nibblers were more than halfway through.

We had only minutes left. A ripple of fear went through me. "Maybe someone else could pop out from under the bed and rescue us?"

"Nice plan, Jack," Cherry said, "but who?"

"Maybe me!" said a cheery voice from under Clyde's bed, and next moment Sunil appeared on the other side of Cherry. He was still wearing her spare goggles and brandishing my extra torch. "Where are the monsters?"

"On the ropes!" I told him. "Quickly!"

He flicked on the torch and swung round, sweeping the beam over the cheesy toe nibblers – first on Clyde's rope, then Cherry's, then mine. I sighed with relief as the toe nibblers vanished, and hoped Sunil couldn't see how I was shaking.

"How'd you find us?" Cherry asked. She was clearly as bemused as me. "How did you get here?"

"You kidding?" came another voice, gruffer but even more welcome than Sunil's. "We just followed that 'Eeeeeeeee! Eeeeeeeee!' noise!"

"Bernard!" Cherry and I chorused in relief.

"EEEEEEEEEEEE!" Clyde added.

"Shut *up*, Clyde!" I said.

"Don't say that, Jack!" Bernard exclaimed, wriggling out from under the bed as soon as Sunil snapped the torch off, and standing up. "I love that sound – it's music to my ears! And don't crack any jokes about the ears," he added, unfurling them.

"EEEEEEEEEEEEE!" said Clyde. "Mr Bun!!! *MR BUN!!!*"

"You've got lousy taste in music, Bernard," Cherry said. "If you *have* to listen to that stuff, can't you use headphones?" She paused for a second, as if playing back what she'd just said. "Oh, terrific. As if being tied to a skatebed ready to be catapulted into the air as part of an evil monster master plan wasn't bad enough, now I'm turning into my mum."

My bed juddered, and my stomach followed suit. "Can we cut the chit-chat and get us out of these beds?" I snapped. "These ropes might not hold us much longer."

"I came prepared!" Sunil said earnestly, fishing in his backpack and – after what seemed like ages – producing a tiny little penknife. He opened it up and started sawing feebly at the tough leathery straps that held Cherry.

Just at that moment Clyde's bed shook as a strand of his rope parted. "EEEEEEEEEEEEE! EEEEEEEEEEEEEEE!" he commented.

"Come on, Bernard," I said anxiously. "Get to work! Cut the straps!"

"What with?" Bernard asked. "I don't have a knife!"

Clyde's bed shook again, inching forward as another strand of rope parted. Moments later, so did mine, twice in quick succession.

"Try biting them!" I yelled.

"What, with these tiny little teeth?" Bernard demanded, peeling back his lips.

"They're better than nothing!"

Bernard shrugged, and leaned over Clyde. "EEEEE EEEEEEEEEEE EEEEEEEEEE EEEEEEEEEEE EEEEEEEE EEEEEEEEEEE EEEEEE EEEEEEE

EEEEEEE EEEEEE EEEEEEEEEE EEEEEEEEEEEE!" Clyde shrieked. "EEEEEEEEEEEEEEEEEEEEE EEEE!"

SNICK! Two long, sharp-looking bunny-fangs suddenly shot out from under Bernard's upper lip – proper, serious, monstery rabbit teeth. A look of joyous, if slightly goofy, disbelief came over his face.

"Wild!" he grinned.

"*EEEEEEEEEEEEEEEEEEEEE!!!*" added Clyde, as Bernard set to work, gnawing away at the straps. In a matter of moments, he'd chewed through the first one and started on the second.

"Whoa!" Cherry exclaimed as a couple of frayed strands broke and her bed lurched. Sunil sawed more frantically. He was doing his best, but at that rate it was going to take him a week to get through just one strap. And we didn't have a week. By my reckoning, we had maybe three minutes. I could feel a creaking and twanging through the bed frame as the fibres of my own rope continued to unravel and snap, one by one.

"Hurry, Bernard!" I said urgently.

"I'm going as fast as I can!" Bernard said, his mouth full of strap – so actually, it was more like, "Mmmm gng ff fffffff ff ng ng!" but I knew what he meant.

Moments later, the strap gave way and Clyde's hands were free. This was not a good thing. He sat up and, screaming hysterically, started pounding on Bernard's head as Bernard worked on the next strap.

"Don't be such an idiot, Clyde!" I roared, fear feeding my anger. "He's trying to help you!"

"*EEEEEEEEEEEEEEEEEEEE!!!*" Clyde replied, hammering frantically at Bernard.

"Mr Bernard! Quickly!" Sunil shouted, suddenly and desperately, as several strands of the rope – the only thing that was stopping Cherry from shooting up the ramp and over the wall – parted at once. Her skatebed lurched forward, jerked; more strands snapped; the rope held, but only just.

Bernard strained at the half-chewed strap round Clyde's ankles. It snapped; Clyde scurried off the bed and fled to a corner of the chamber where, still making that "Eeeeee! Eeeeee!" noise, he tried to dig his way out using his shoulder blades. Bernard whirled and started on the straps that held Cherry.

The little creaks and twangs through the bed frame were constant now. My rope was almost gone. But the rope holding Cherry was in an even worse state; I couldn't afford to distract Bernard while he was helping her.

The strap at Cherry's ankles had been bitten through, and Bernard was working on the next one. He was through it in seconds and onto the third, but the vibrations of the rope snapping, strand by strand, were really scaring me now. Bernard chewed, quickly and steadily. The bed juddered; lurched; jerked a little closer to the ramp. Bernard redoubled his efforts; in moments he was onto the fourth strap.

With a whip-like, tearing sound and an elastic *twang!!!* from the bungee, the rope holding Clyde's empty skatebed gave way. The bed took off like a frightened rabbit with a jet-propelled wolf on its tail, shooting off the end of the ramp and somersaulting clumsily over the wall to land with a crash on the other side. There was a roar; more terrible slurping sounds;

a furious banging and crashing; and then something was flung back onto our side of the wall.

It was the frame of the skatebed, twisted out of all recognition by something horribly strong.

All this had taken less time than it took Bernard to get through the fourth strap. Gently but urgently, he nudged Sunil aside and grabbed the final strap from him, pulling at where the penknife had been working on it. Cherry's bed shuddered again.

So did mine.

Bernard bent and closed his new teeth on the damaged strap. The strain showed on his face as he wrenched at it. It parted.

So did the rope, cracking like a whip. Bernard just had time to grab Cherry before the bed was whisked out from under her and hurled up the ramp towards the wall.

My heart was pounding with fear. The bed shuddered and jerked wildly as another strand of rope tore, and another, and another. "Hurry, Bernard," I muttered again under my breath.

Setting Cherry down, Bernard spun, ready to release me. But it was already too late. I heard Cherry shout, "No!" as the rope snapped.

The bungee pulled. The skatebed took off. I was flung helplessly up the ramp towards certain doom.

Over the wall, the hideous slurping sounds began again.

The room blurred around me as the bed accelerated up the ramp. I could hear Cherry yelling something; Sunil shouting; the hideous noises as the hidden monsters tore Cherry's skatebed apart. And above it all, the piercing sound of Clyde's shrieking. I think I might have screamed, too.

Everything seemed to go into slow motion as the bed hit the top of the ramp and the straps released automatically. Suddenly I was in freefall, hurtling through space towards the wall and the creatures beyond. The darkness flickered strangely around me, with a sound like distant thunder.

There was a haze of movement in the corner of my eye. Something crossed my path, filled my vision – something large and covered in downy feathers. With an "Ooomph!" I hit it, its softness cushioning the impact; two strong arms folded gently around me. I could see nothing, but I felt us fall.

Next thing I knew, I was easing myself into a sitting position – still on the safe side of the wall, between it and the ramp, with Cherry and Sunil looking anxiously down at me. The skatebed stood nearby, its bungee trailing limply. Beneath me, there was something large and soft and warm.

"Um . . . Jack?" Bernard said. "You can get off me now."

I looked down into his grumpy buck-toothed face and almost laughed with relief. "Thanks, Bernard," I said. "I owe you one."

"You owe me several dozen, kid," he growled. Then he winked. "Now get off, OK?"

"That was amazing, Bernard!" Cherry said. "How'd you do that?"

"Yeah!" Sunil agreed. "I didn't think anyone could jump that high! It was amazing! You just jumped up and caught Jack like you were the best basketball player in the world!"

Shakily, I stood and looked up at the top of the ramp. I couldn't see how Bernard had leaped that high either. "And what's with the teeth?" I added.

Bernard grinned as he sat up. "Neat, huh? And watch this!" With a *SNICK!* the teeth withdrew behind his upper lip.

SNICK! They shot out again. Another *SNICK!* and they were back out of sight.

"Wow!" murmured Sunil. "Cool!"

"I didn't know you could do that!" Cherry said.

"Neither did I." Bernard grinned. "And I've never jumped like that in my life before. But right now, I feel like I've been supercharged!"

"What with?" I asked.

Bernard swung round and pointed at Clyde, who was just pausing for breath. "Fear," he said. "Pure, one hundred per cent A-grade fear, straight from the source."

Clyde looked up and saw Bernard pointing at him. "*EEEEEE!!!*" he said. "*EEEEEEEEEEEEEEEEEEEE!!!*"

"The source?" Sunil asked, puzzled.

"*My* source," Bernard said. "Monsters are created from the fears of children – and I was made from *his* fear. The fears of your source child – the child whose fears made you in the first place – well, there's nothing else like that. Nothing like it in the world. All that 'EEEEEEEEE!' stuff he's been doing – that's what charged me up. That's what made me strong, and gave me these cool teeth." He *SNICK*ed them out and in again, just for fun. "Man! I feel *so* good!" He did a funky wiggly dance around us. "*SO* good!" He glanced down at himself. "Do I look taller to you?"

Cherry looked at me. "What now?"

Sunil butted in. "Now? We go home, don't we?"

I wished we could. I *so* wished we could. But we had work to do. I shook my head, but the words wouldn't come.

"We've got to take care of Mr Whisper," Cherry said, filling Sunil and Bernard in on what they'd missed.

Bernard whistled.

"Wow," he said. "What kind of weirdo kid must *his* source child be?"

I wondered the same. Most kids were frightened of things – spiders, snakes, toy bunny rabbits, unusual wallpaper, creatures that had too many heads or eyes or legs, or that nibbled your toes or made spooky noises. There had to be a kid somewhere who was afraid of noses, or at least of one nose, which would explain Augustus.

But Whisper wasn't like that. It was as if Whisper was born from the fears of someone who knew about monsters – someone who was afraid that one day he'd meet a monster that was too smart for him, that always thought ahead, that couldn't be beaten by the usual methods.

My blood froze. Suddenly, I knew exactly what kind of kid was afraid of meeting a monster like that. More, I knew exactly *who* was afraid of meeting a monster like that. I knew who was Whisper's source child – the child whose fears had called him into being.

It was me.

"I don't know," Sunil was saying. "This all sounds a bit dangerous to me. Why can't you let someone else deal with it?"

"There isn't anybody else," I said, standing. My legs felt like wet jelly, and in my stomach a whole family of butterflies were trying to dig their way out using a blunt spoon, but I knew now: this was up to me. Mr Whisper was *my* monster. I didn't know if I could beat him – I didn't know if anyone could – but I had to try.

Then another thought struck me. "Did

anyone else notice the darkness flickering – and hear a thundery noise? Just before Bernard saved me?"

Cherry worked it out at once. "Of course!" she exclaimed. "Part one of Whisper's plan! When Jack thought he was going over the wall, it powered up the Depth Charge for the first time – and blew the barriers. The Dark Depths really are open now. Wide open."

This was bad with a capital B. Worse, it was bad with a capital everything. Even letters that don't belong in 'bad' were putting on their capital coats and crowding in there.

"I reckon it's been almost five minutes since then," I said. "We have to assume that the monsters from the Dark Depths are out in the monster underworld; but if we're lucky, none of them will have made it to the human world yet. We've got to try and stop them."

"OK," Bernard said, "you and Cherry get on the case. I'll deal with this Whisper guy."

I shook my head. "Whisper's mine."

"But—" Bernard began.

"No," I said. "I mean he's *really* mine. He's my monster. Remember, Cherry? He didn't say the Depth Charge would be powered by *our* fears; he said it would be powered by *my* fears."

"Hold on, Jack," Bernard said. "Are you telling me . . . ?"

I nodded. "I'm his source child. Think about it, Bernard. It's the only explanation – otherwise, why would he bother trying to frighten me when he's got Clyde there going 'EEEEEEEEEEEEEEEE!' non-stop?

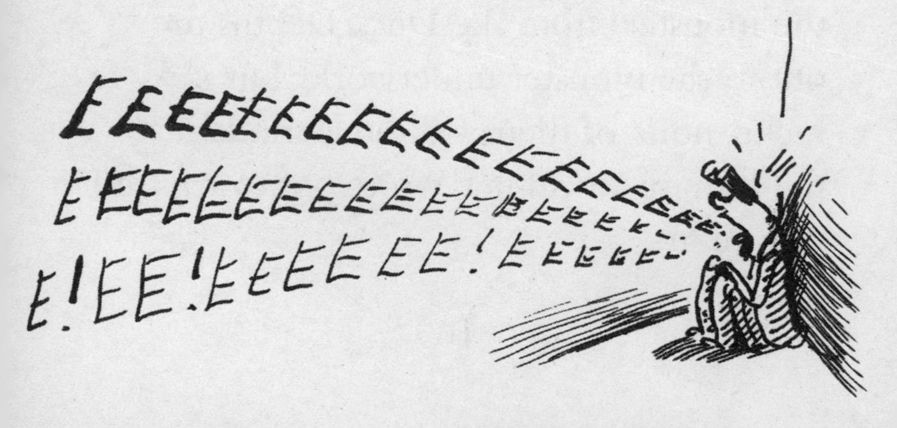

That's why it's got to be me who deals with him. If I don't, he'll never leave me alone."

"Anyway," Cherry added to Bernard, "without you, we can't get back to the monster underworld."

"Yeah," Bernard said, "but—"

"Not now, Bernard. There's no time to discuss things," I told him. "Right now, there could be monsters from the Dark Depths appearing under beds all over the place. Can you do something to stop them?"

"Sure," he admitted. "If something like that shows up, any kid's going to give off a fear signal you could read from the moon. I'll just follow the signal and wrestle the monster back to the underworld."

Cherry looked dismayed. "Wrestle a monster from the Dark Depths? Bernard, are you sure?"

He grinned. "Right now, I feel so pumped I could wrestle one with my ears!"

"Anyway," I said, "it's only for ten

minutes – as long as we can stop the Depth Charge exploding."

"But just to be safe," Bernard said, "I'll do a quick recharge." He turned towards Clyde, who was taking a breather from screaming and putting in some gentle sobbing time in the corner. "BOO!" he roared. *SNICK!* went Bernard's new teeth.

"*EEEEEEEEEEE EEEEEE EEEEEEEEEEEEEEEE!!!*" went Clyde. "*EEEEEEEEE EEEEEEEEEEEE EEEEEEEEEEEEEEEE EEEEEEE!!!*"

Bernard basked in the scream like a vertical sunbather. Somehow, he *did* seem to be getting bigger, or more muscular, or something. Then, with a wink and a wave, he dived for the space under the one remaining skatebed. "Meet you back here in ten minutes!" he called as he disappeared.

Clyde fainted. I think he'd forgotten to breathe in. Suddenly, everything was silent. Dead silent.

"Sunil," I said, "you stay here and look after Clyde. Cherry, you stay here and look after Sunil—"

"No!" Cherry cut me off. "No way, Jack. I'm coming in with you."

"Cherry," I began, "this is my responsibility. Whisper's my monster, made from my fears . . ."

"Yeah, yeah, and you've got to face your fears. But you don't have to face them alone." She moved to the corner where our stuff was piled and picked up the Night Blaster. "I'm not letting you go in there by yourself."

I could tell from her expression that she wasn't going to be talked out of this. "You realize these may not work against Whisper?" I said, as she handed me my torch and Freddy the Teddy.

She shrugged. "Then we'll find something that does. Ain't no monster that's a match for the world's greatest Monster Investigator – or her best friend, either." She grinned, and somehow, just for a moment, I felt better.

Then the fear lurched back into my stomach as I opened the door and strode out to face Mr Whisper.

The chamber was darker than before. That strange darker darkness of the Dark Depths had darkened the room until it was so dark that however many times you said the word 'dark' it still wouldn't explain exactly *how* darkly dark the dark darkness was.

The huge bulk of the Depth Charge rose high above us like an enormous foot, ready to stamp down hard. I shivered. The family of butterflies in my stomach had found a hammer and were swinging it around wildly.

Of Mr Whisper there was no sign.

"Where is he, do you think?" Cherry murmured.

I shrugged and switched on my torch,

sweeping the beam around the chamber. Nothing showed up in its light.

"No sign of him," I said.

"Why would he leave?" Cherry puzzled. "His evil master plan's only half-finished."

"Maybe he just popped to the loo."

Cherry shook her head. "Evil masterminds don't leave their doomsday devices unguarded while they pop to the loo," she said. "Do monsters need the loo, anyway?"

I shrugged. "Remind me to ask Bernard. Hey – maybe we should look for the 'off' switch."

I swung the torch-beam up at the Depth Charge.

It looked down at me and grinned nastily.

I almost dropped my torch in shock.

It was Whisper, grown somehow to enormous size and standing right in front of the Depth Charge, hiding it from view. I tried to shout out, to warn Cherry, but fear grabbed hold of my tongue; next moment, Whisper had reached down to grab hold of her.

"Cherry!" Just in time, I found my voice

Cherry looked up, sprang, rolled out of reach and came up with the Night Blaster on and pointed right in Whisper's face. I stood frozen, while the butterflies in my stomach set to work with a pneumatic drill. I was vaguely aware of the Depth Charge whirring and whining back into life.

Whisper laughed, a cold, unpleasant sound that echoed in the vast cavern. "I'm afraid not, Miss Jackson," he said mockingly, the brightness of the Night Blaster lighting his face up like a full moon. "The truth is, you can't defeat me. I am unbeatable!"

"No one's unbeatable, Whisper!" I said, my voice shaking with fear.

"Not even you, eh, Jack? That's what you've always been afraid of, isn't it? That, one day, someone will beat you. Well, now your fears have come true. I *have* beaten you. And even if it takes a little longer than I'd planned, your fear *will* power my Depth Charge. The Dark Depths *will* be destroyed. And—"

"Yeah, yeah, yeah," Cherry interrupted. "And you will rule the world! We've done that. Now, you're a monster, this is a torch; hurry up and disappear, would you?"

Quick as a flash, Whisper grabbed for her again. This time, he didn't miss. The Night Blaster fell from her hand as she was snatched high into the air; it struck the ground, its light blinking once and then vanishing. Only the beam from my own torch remained.

"Run, Jack!" Cherry shouted. "Get out of here!"

I stood firm, though now the butterflies seemed to have got a couple of bulldozers from somewhere and were racing them round inside me. But alongside the fear, there was a new and sudden anger. And with the anger came a fresh thought.

Why had Whisper grabbed Cherry and not me?

Could it be that he couldn't?

I thought about it, my mind racing furiously. He'd grabbed Cherry, he'd kidnapped Clyde, but he'd never so much as laid a finger on me. OK, so I'd been strapped to a bed and almost catapulted over a wall, but even then Whisper hadn't actually touched me. None of that would have happened at all if I hadn't made some pretty serious mistakes.

And I wouldn't have made the mistakes if I'd been thinking clearly.

Why wasn't I thinking clearly? Because I was afraid. Mr Whisper had made me afraid, and then he'd used my fear to trap me.

Well, enough was enough. Whisper was threatening my friend, and I couldn't afford to let him harm her. Suddenly, I knew what I had to do.

I had to face my fears.

"OK, Whisper," I said, levelling the torch-beam at him. "It's time to end this. Face me like a monster."

Whisper chuckled. "Really, Jack. Do you think your torch will suddenly be able to hurt me?"

I shook my head. "You're right, Whisper. I can't rely on my torch." I switched it off and put it down. "Or my teddy." I gave Freddy a gentle kiss

Kiss

on top of his head and set him down next to the torch. Was it my imagination, or did Whisper's face, made pale green by the night vision goggles, suddenly look a little less sure of itself? "It's just you and me, Whisper."

I took one last look at Cherry, still held tight in Whisper's fist. Then I took off my night vision goggles and put them, too, on the floor.

"Are you sure you want to do this, Jack?" Whisper's voice hissed through the darkness; but he was the one who sounded less sure; less confident; less dangerous. It gave me the hope I needed to fight against my fear, and as I stepped forward I heard the whine of the Depth Charge wind down and fade away. Even the butterflies in my stomach fell still, as if they were waiting to see what would happen.

Now there was just me, Whisper, the darkness and the silence.

"Don't be silly, Jack," Whisper's voice said from out of the darkness, as I took another step forward. "You can't beat me. I'm smarter than you."

A tingle of fear ran up my spine. I chased it back down. "Maybe you are," I said as I stepped forward again. "But I'm not going to let you scare me any more." I took another step forward. "And even if you do scare me, I'm not going to let being scared bother me." Another step. "So let's finish this now, and if you're going to do anything to me, do it. Otherwise, leave me alone!"

And with that, I marched

forward. I didn't care any more; I really didn't. I'd finally realized that the worst bit of all of this was being scared. It was like the time at school when one of the big kids was threatening to hit me. I spent three weeks being frightened to go to school, and when he finally did hit me, it wasn't so bad. I mean, it hurt; but being hurt once like that was better than being scared for three whole weeks had been. A lot better.

Part of me wondered if Whisper might do something a lot worse than just hit me, but I pressed that thought down again and kept going.

And going.

And going.

Just when I was beginning to wonder where he was, I walked into the wall.

"Ow!" I said.

"Here, Jack," said a voice from just behind me. "You might want to put these back on."

And Cherry handed me my night vision goggles.

I slipped them on, and could hardly believe what I saw. Cherry was standing there, safe and grinning, and clasped in her hand . . .

. . . was Mr Whisper. A very tiny Mr Whisper, glaring at me.

"Don't be fooled, Jack!" he squeaked. "This is all part of my plan! I've out-thought you all the way, and—"

I leaned my face in close to his. "Shut up," I told him firmly. "I'm not afraid of you any more."

He shrank away from me, quite literally.

"Careful, Jack," Cherry said. "You keep doing that, there'll be nothing left of him!"

I smiled at her, my first real smile for hours. "See if I care!" I said. "Let's go check on Sunil and Clyde."

"No need," Cherry told me. "Here they come!"

Sunil and Clyde were fine – or at least, Sunil was fine and Clyde was Clyde, which was the best that could be hoped for. They'd got fed up waiting, and come to see how we were doing. That is, Sunil had. Clyde was too scared to stay by himself, so he'd tagged along, snivelling quietly.

We had a lot to tell them; but first we had to find somewhere safe to put little Mr Whisper. Cherry handed him to me while she searched her Mr Piggy backpack. It felt a bit creepy holding him – especially as he kept wriggling and squeaking – but it was bearable. Anyway, pretty soon Cherry found the perfect container – a pink sparkly Magic Fairy pencil case.

"Don't ask," she growled, as she unzipped it and we put Whisper inside, ignoring his pleas for mercy. "It's not mine, OK?"

"So how did he get to be so small?"

Sunil asked.

"Oh, man, Jack was amazing!" Cherry said proudly, and she launched into an account of everything that had happened.

"So," Sunil said slowly, after she'd finished, "when Jack faced his fears, they got smaller. Is that it?"

"More or less," I agreed.

Clyde suddenly perked up. "Wait a minute!" he said. "If you can do that to your monster – I can do it to mine!"

Cherry and I exchanged a worried glance. "Hang on, Clyde," I said, "Bernard's one of the good guys!"

"Yeah, Clyde, we need him!" Cherry put in. "You can't—"

But Clyde wasn't listening.

"Yes!" he said excitedly. "I can do that! I can be brave! Next time Mr Bun comes to scare me, I'll just stand up, and look him in the eye, and say, 'You don't scare me, Mr Bun! Clear off!' And then when he gets smaller, I'll stick my tongue out at him and call him names, and when he gets really small I'll zip him up in a teddy-bear pyjama case!"

"Just try it, kid!" growled a deep voice behind him.

Clyde spun round.

"Boo!" said Bernard.

"*EEEEEEEEEEEEEEEEEEEE EEEEEEEEEEEEEEEEEEEEEEE EEEEEEEEEEEEEEEEEEEEEEE EEEE!!!*" said Clyde, and fainted again.

Bernard grinned. "I don't think I've got anything to worry about," he said.

"Are you sure, Bernard?" I asked, taking a step backwards. "What's that under your arm?"

He looked down at the enormous creature that was wriggling uncomfortably in the crook of his elbow. Imagine a gigantic hosepipe with a head like a claw hammer and a face made of nuts and bolts

and you'll get the picture.

"This thing? It's just a monster from the Dark Depths. They ain't so bad once you beat 'em in a fair fight. I'm getting quite fond of this one – think I might keep it. I'm going to call it Gerald."

The hammerheaded hosepipey thing writhed and hissed venomously at him.

Bernard cuffed it across the nose. "Hey," he went on, looking up at the Depth Charge, "I guess this must be that machine of Whisper's you were telling me about."

I nodded. "I don't think it can do any harm now," I said, "but I'm not sure we should just leave it here."

"No problem!" said Bernard, and before we could say anything he was whirling Gerald around by the tail.

"Mr Bernard!" Sunil scolded. "That's no way to treat a pet!"

"This is a monster!" Bernard said cheerfully. "And this," he added, swinging Gerald hammerhead-first into the Depth Charge, "is a monster's idea of fun!" There was a tremendous **CRASH!** as the great machine folded in half. Again Bernard swung Gerald, and again and again, the hammerhead whiplashing into the metal and pounding it flat until the Depth Charge was nothing but a twisted pile of junk lying on the floor of the cavern.

Bernard stood there, panting and dangling the enormous hammerheaded hosepipey thing from one paw.

"Man, that felt good!" he said, smiling from ear to ear.

"But it wasn't very kind to Gerald," Sunil told him. "A pet is for life, not just for utterly destroying an evil monster mastermind's doomsday machine."

Gerald hissed at him. Then it looked

up adoringly at Bernard and said, "More! More!"

Bernard winked cheerily. "Mission accomplished!" he said. "The Dark Depths are all closed up again; the scary monsters are back where they belong; and the Depth Charge is all mashed up. And, man, Jack – the way you fixed Whisper: that was incredible!"

"You saw that?" I asked.

"Sure!" he said. "I'd just wrestled Gerald into submission when its time ran out and it got dragged back here. I got dragged back with it. Got here just in time to see you facing down Whisper with no goggles on. Hey – I told you so!"

"You told me what?" I asked, puzzled.

"I told you that one day I'd see what you look like when you're frightened. Well, now I have."

I grinned. "And how do I look?" I asked.

He grinned back. "Scary," he said.

Getting home could have been a problem, but fortunately we still had one skatebed. Of course, there was the worry that maybe some of the monsters from the Dark Depths would learn how to use it to visit the monster underworld, but Bernard solved that one. After he'd taken us home, he went back and climbed over the wall with it.

"I was still so pumped from all of Clyde's screaming," he told me later, "that I knew I'd be fast enough to get out of there before Whisper's monsters got to me. I didn't get much of a look at them before I dived under the bed and back to the monster underworld – but I did see what they'd done to the other skatebed. Believe me,

Jack, no monster's going to be able to use that bed after those guys have finished with it."

We got Clyde home before his parents ever discovered he'd been snatched – not that he showed us any gratitude at all, mind you, but what else is new?

As for Sunil – he may not have had the makings of a Monster Investigator, but he'd helped us out when we needed it and we were truly grateful.

So when we found out how good he is with computers, we had no hesitation in asking him to be our new webmaster. He jumped at the chance.

Of course, he redesigned the site straight away, getting it loads more hits on the search engines in the process. Which means that now we're busier than ever, with kids contacting us all the time to ask for help with their monster problems. Which means that I'm getting even less sleep at night.

But with Mr Whisper locked away inside a sparkly pink Magic Fairy pencil case, inside a Timmy the Train lunchbox, inside a fluffy Magic Rainbow Pony bag, all tied up in a baby's furry My Little Cow blanket, at least my dreams are back to normal – with the monsters losing every time.

Just the way it should be.

JACK SLATER, MONSTER INVESTIGATOR

By John Dougherty

A HILARIOUS TALE OF MONSTERS AND MAYHEM – PERFECT FOR ALL YOUNG ADVENTURE FANS!

Jack Slater is an official Monster Investigator – licensed to hunt out monsters who turn up under beds and terrorize small children (and their parents!). Armed with a high-power torch (monsters hate the light), a pocketful of spare batteries and a much-loved teddy (there is nothing monsters hate more than a favourite childhood toy), he sets off down to Monster Underworld when news reaches his ears that the monsters are on the march. They're getting organized and no-one, not even the Prime Minister in Downing Street, is safe any more . . .

ZEUS ON THE LOOSE!

By John Dougherty

A BRILLIANTLY FUNNY TALE FOR YOUNG READERS ABOUT A GREEK GOD WHO COMES TO LIFE.

"I am the great and mighty Zeus, mortal – give me one good reason why I shouldn't smite you here and now!"

Alex's class are learning about the Ancient Greeks. That's why Alex makes a temple (out of loo rolls and a cornflakes box) for the god Zeus. He doesn't expect the god himself to turn up, borrow his mum's nightie and demand a sacrifice at half-past five in the morning. Even worse, Zeus reckons it's time for another Trojan War – in the school playground!

ZEUS TO THE RESCUE!

By John Dougherty

There's a new girl called Diana in Alex's class and she's causing all sorts of trouble. Ever since she arrived, the girls have been behaving very strangely and Miss Wise is letting them get away with it!

When Alex and Charlie decide to ask the god Zeus for some help, they discover that Diana isn't quite what she seems. And then things start to get even worse. . .

Will Zeus be able to make Miss Wise give him a kiss before it's too late and Alex is turned into a pig?

ZEUS IS ON THE LOOSE . . . AGAIN!

NITERACY HOUR

By John Dougherty

What a louse!

Gregory is a good listener.

Jim is a head-louse, newly-hatched from a nit on Gregory's head.

As school story time turns into Niteracy hour, Jim has breakfast – and becomes a good listener too!

That's how he hears that big, bullying Duncan is going to push Gregory's head down the toilet! Can Jim help Gregory do something about Duncan – the real louse in the class?

NINNYHAMMER

By Dick King-Smith

Peter is a young boy, living on a farm. One day, whilst out doing chores for his father, he comes across a strange white stick floating in the stream. He reaches out and catches it – and finds an exciting new friend in the process.

Ninnyhammer is an outcast in the village, but Peter thinks he's a magician and the white stick is his magic wand. Ninnyhammer is so grateful that he starts to help Peter and his family with their struggling farm – making the sow have more piglets, helping the corn to grow faster and the hens to lay twice as many eggs.

But Peter wants to do something for Ninnyhammer in return. Can it really be right that his friend has to bed down in a hole with foxcubs? And can Peter persuade his dad to help . . . ?

A CLASSIC TALE FROM NATIONAL TREASURE DICK KING-SMITH.

AGENT Z

MEETS THE MASKED CRUSADER

By Mark Haddon

Ben's a born daydreamer. He'd much rather be in the Sahara, or on a Viking ship, than sitting in a boring maths lesson. Then Agent Z appears on the scene – and THAT means secret missions, cunning plans and careful strategies. And soon Ben and his friends, Barney and Jenks, realize that life on planet Earth is rather exciting after all!

'Slipping effortlessly between reality and a rich fantasy world, this is breathless action from start to finish.'
The Guardian